Give Them Unquiet Dreams

———

James Mulhern

ISBN: 9781082240621

Dedication

For Brother Mike, and for Brother Mark, whose spirit is always
beside me

*The distinction between the past, present, and future
is only a stubbornly persistent illusion.*
—Albert Einstein

Acknowledgments

The Irish people, the living and the dead,
their literature and their laughter.
And immigrants, who have always made America great.

The distance that the dead have gone does not at first appear—Their
coming back seems possible for many an ardent year.
—Emily Dickinson

Chapter One

When I was a child, my grandmother gave me advice that I've been turning over in my mind ever since. "Never forget where you came from." So I remember my origins. I am borne back ceaselessly into the past.

Nana sat on the toilet seat. I was on the floor in front of her.

She brushed my brown curly hair until my scalp hurt.

"You have your grandfather's hair. Stand up. Look at yourself in the mirror."

I touched my scalp. "It hurts."

"You must toughen up, Aiden. Weak people get nowhere in this world. Your grandfather was weak. Addicted to the bottle. Your mother has an impaired mind. Now she's in a nuthouse. And your father, he couldn't handle the responsibility of a child. People have to be strong. Do you understand me?" She bent and stared into my face. Her hazel eyes seemed enormous. I smelled coffee on her breath. There were blackheads on her nose. She pinched my cheeks.

I reflexively pushed her hands away.

"Life is full of pain, sweetheart. And I don't mean just the physical kind." She took a cigarette from her case on the back of the toilet, lit it, and inhaled. "You'll be hurt a lot, but you must carry on.

You know what the British people used to say when the Germans bombed London during World War Two?"

"No."

"Keep calm and carry on." She hit my backside. "Now run along and put some clothes on." I was wearing my underwear and T-shirt. "We have a busy day."

I dressed in the jeans and a yellow short-sleeve shirt she had bought me. She stood in front of the mirror by the front door of the living room, arranging her pearl necklace. She put on bright red lipstick and fingered her gray hair, trying to hide a thinning spot at the top of her forehead. She turned and smoothed her green cotton dress, glancing at herself from behind. "Not bad for an old broad." She looked me over. "Come here." She tucked my shirt in, licked her hand, and smoothed my hair. "You'd think I never brushed it."

As she opened the front door, she said, "Hold on," and went to the kitchen counter and put her hand in a glass jar full of bills. She took out at least thirty single dollar bills.

"Here. Give this money to the kiddos next door."

When we were outside, she pushed me toward their house. They were playing on their swing set in the fenced-in yard. In front of the broken-down house was a yard of weeds. A rusted bicycle with no wheels lay on the ground. The pale girl with limp dirty hair looked at me suspiciously as I approached the fence. Her brother stood, arms folded, in the background. He scowled and spit.

"This is for you," I said, shoving the money through the chain links. The girl reached out to grab it, but most of the bills fell onto the dirt.

"Thank you," she said.

As I walked away, her brother yelled, "We don't need no charity from you."

I opened the door of my grandmother's blue Plymouth. The air-conditioning blasted, and the interior was full of cigarette smoke.

She crossed herself. "Say it with me. 'There but for the grace of God go I.'"

I repeated the words with her, and we drove to her friend Margie's house. Margie was a smelly fat lady with a big white cat that hissed at me. She always wore the same navy-blue sweater and was constantly picking cat hairs off her clothes while talking about the latest sermon, God, or the devil. Nana told me when Margie was a young girl, her classmates made fun of her. "Smelly," they called her. And she did smell. Like urine, cats, and mothballs.

"Don't let him get out," Margie yelled as the cat pounced from behind the open door. "Arthur, don't you dare run out!" She bent to grab his tail and groaned. "My back!"

"Don't worry. I got him." I had my arms wrapped around the white monster. He hissed.

"Why don't you put him in the closet when you open the front door? We go through this every time." My grandmother pushed past her toward the kitchen in the back of the house. "I have to sit down. It's hot as a pig's arse out there."

Margie placed a tray of ham sandwiches, along with cheese and crackers, on the round gray Formica table. I liked her wallpaper—yellow with the red outlines of children holding hands in circles. On the back wall, she had pinned an American Flag with a sign underneath that read, "Happy Birthday, America. 1776—1976."

"I don't know how I feel about all those miracles Father Flynn was going on about." Margie placed a sandwich on a plate for me with some chips. "What ya want to drink, Aiden? I got nice lemonade." Her two front teeth were red from where her lipstick had smudged. As usual, cat hairs covered her blue sweater, especially the ledge of her belly where the cat must have sat all the time.

"That sounds good."

She smiled. "Always such a nice boy. Polite. You'll never have any trouble with this one. Not like you did with Lorraine."

"I hate when you call her that."

"That's her name, ain't it?" She poured my grandmother and me lemonade and sat with a huff.

"That was my mother's name, her formal name. I prefer to call my daughter Laura."

"What the hell difference does it make?" Margie bit into her sandwich and rolled her eyes at me.

"Makes a lot of difference. My mother was a strange woman. I named my daughter Lorraine out of respect for the dead."

"Laura is . . ." I knew Margie was going to say that my mother was strange too.

"Laura is what?" My grandmother put her sandwich on her plate and leaned in to Margie.

"Is a nice girl. She's got problems, but don't we all?" She reached out and clasped my hand. "Right, Aiden?"

"Yes, Margie."

My grandmother rubbed her neck and spoke softly. "Nobody's perfect. Laura's getting better. She's got a few psychological issues. The new meds seem to be helping. She's the most gentle, optimistic person I've ever known. Didn't even argue when we said it was best for her to spend some time at McCall's." Her eyes were shiny and her face flushed. Her bottom lip trembled. She looked at me. "Don't you need to use the bathroom?" She raised her eyebrows. That was her signal.

"Yes, I gotta pee."

"You don't have to be so detailed," she said. "Just go."

Margie laughed hard and farted.

I exited and crept up the gray stairs. The old bannister was dusty. The rug in the upstairs hall was full of Arthur's hair. I picked up a piece to examine it, then rubbed my pants. Nana said Margie's room was the last one on the left. Her jewelry case was on top of her dresser. I took the diamond earrings and opal bracelet Nana had told me about. There were also a couple of showy rings—one a large red stone, the other a blue one. These and a gold necklace with a cross I shoved into my pockets. Then I walked to the bathroom and flushed the toilet. I messed up the towel a bit so it looked like I dried my hands.

When I entered the kitchen, they were still talking about miracles.

My grandmother passed our plates to Margie, who had filled the sink with sudsy water.

"He raised Lazarus from the dead," Margie said. "And then he healed the deaf and dumb men. And the blind man too," she said raising her hand and splashing my grandmother.

"Let's not forget about the fish. And the water into wine," my grandmother said.

Margie shook her head. "I don't know, Catherine." She looked into the sink. "It's hard to believe that Jesus could have done all that. Why aren't there miracles today?" I imagined a trout springing from the frothy bubbles.

My grandmother smiled at me. "Of course there are miracles today. As a matter of fact, I'm taking Aiden to that priest at Mission Church. A charismatic healer is what they call him. Aiden's going to be cured, aren't you, honey?"

"Cured of what?" Margie said.

"He's got a little something wrong with his blood is all. Too many white cells. Leukemia. This priest will take care of all that."

"Leukemia!" Margie said. "Catherine, that's serious." Margie tried to smile at me, but I could tell she was upset. "Sit down, honey." She motioned for me to go to the table. "We're almost done here."

"You gotta take him to a good doctor," she whispered to my grandmother, as if I couldn't hear.

"I know that. I'm not a *stook*."

"What's a stork gotta do with this?"

"An Irish expression. Means idiot."

We said our goodbyes, and when we were in the car, my grandmother said, "Let me see what you have." I pulled the goods out of my pockets while she unclasped her black plastic pocketbook. Her eyes lit up.

"Perfect. She isn't watching, is she?" I looked at the house. Margie was nowhere in sight. Probably sitting on her rocking chair with Arthur in her lap.

"Put those in here." She nodded toward her bag.

When we were about to turn onto Tremont Street where the church was, I remembered the gold necklace and cross. I pulled it out of my pocket, and my grandmother took it from me, running a red light. "This would look beautiful on Laura." In a moment, a police car blaring sirens followed us.

"Don't say anything." My grandmother moved to the side of the road. She looked in the rearview mirror and rolled her window down.

"Ma'am, you ran a red light." The policeman was tall with a hooked nose and dark brown close-set eyes.

"I know, Officer. I was saying a prayer with my grandson. He gave me this gold cross. I got distracted. I'm very sorry."

He leaned into the car. I smiled.

"Is that a birthday gift for your grandmother?"

"Yes. I wanted to surprise her."

"And he certainly did," she said, patting my knee and smiling at the police officer.

"It's good no cars were coming. You could have been hurt," he said. "That's a beautiful cross," he added.

My grandmother began to cry. "Isn't it, though?" She sniffled.

The officer placed his hand firmly on the edge of the window. "Consider this a warning. You can go. I'd put that cross away."

"Of course. Of course." She turned to me. "Here, Aiden. Put it back in your pocket."

The police officer waited for us to drive off. I turned and looked. He waved.

"Are you sad, Nana?"

"Don't be silly." She waved her hand. "That was an act."

We laughed.

We parked and entered Mission Church. It smelled of shellac, incense, perfume, and old people. It was hard to see in the musty darkness. Bright light shone through the stained-glass windows where Jesus was depicted in the Stations of the Cross.

"Let's move to the front." My grandmother pulled me out of the line and cut in front of an old lady, who looked bewildered.

"Shouldn't you go to the end of the line?" she whispered, smiling down at me. Her hair was sweaty, and her freckled fat bicep jiggled when she tapped my grandmother's shoulder. I thought of the asteroid belt.

"I'm sorry. We're in a hurry. We have to help a sick neighbor after this. I want my grandson to get a cure."

"What's wrong?" the woman whispered. We were four people away from the priest, who was standing at the altar. He prayed over people then lightly touched them. They fell backward into the arms of two old men with maroon suit jackets and blue ties.

"Aiden has leukemia."

The woman's eyes teared up. "I'm sorry." She patted my forearm. Again, her flabby bicep jiggled, and the asteroids bounced.

When it was our turn, my grandmother said, "Father, please cure him. And can you say a prayer for my daughter too?"

"Of course." The silver-haired, red-faced priest bent down. I smelled alcohol on his breath. "What ails you, young man?"

I was confused.

"He's asking you about your illness, Aiden."

"I have leukemia," I said proudly.

The priest said some mumbo-jumbo prayer and pushed my chest. I knew I was supposed to fall back but was afraid the old geezers wouldn't catch me.

"Fall," my grandmother whispered irritably. Then she said extra softly, "Remember our plan."

I fell hard, shoving myself against the old guy. He toppled over as well. People gasped. His friend and the priest began to pick us up. I pretended to be hurt badly. "Ow. My head is killing me."

Several people gathered around us. My grandmother yelled "Oh my God" and stepped onto the altar, kneeling in front of a giant crucified Jesus. "Dear Jesus," she said loudly, "I don't know how many more tribulations I can take." Then she crossed herself, hurried across the altar, and put a gold chalice in her handbag. My moaning and fake crying distracted everyone.

"He'll be OK." She put her arm under mine and helped the others raise me.

When I was standing, she said to the priest, "You certainly have the power of the Holy Spirit in you. It came out of you like the water gushing from the rock at Rephidim and Kadesh.

"Let's get out of here before there's a flood." She laughed. The priest looked confused. The old lady who let us cut in line eyed my grandmother's handbag and shook her head as we passed.

When we were in front of Rita's house, our last stop before home, I asked my grandmother what *tribulation* meant. And where were *Repapah* and *Kadiddle*?

She laughed. "You pronounced those places wrong, but it doesn't matter. Your mother used to do the same thing whenever I quoted that Bible passage and she'd ask me where they were too." She opened the car door. "I don't know where the hell those places are. Somewhere in the Middle East . . . And a tribulation is a problem."

"Oh."

After ringing the doorbell a couple of times, we opened the door. We found Rita passed out on the couch.

My grandmother took an ice cube from the freezer and held it against her forehead. Rita sat bolt upright. "You scared the bejesus out of me." She was wearing a yellow nightgown, and her auburn hair was set in curlers. "Aiden, I didn't see you there." She kissed my cheek. For the second time that day, I smelled alcohol.

"Do you think you can help me out?" my grandmother asked. Rita looked at me.

"Of course I can."

"Pull me up and I'll get my checkbook." I realized all my grandmother's friends were fat.

At the kitchen table, Rita said, "Should I make it out to the hospital?"

"Make it out to me. I've opened a bank account to pay for his medical expenses."

"Will five thousand do?" Rita was rich. Her husband was a "real-estate tycoon," my grandmother was always saying. He dropped dead shoveling snow a few years back.

"That's so generous of you." My grandmother cried again. More fake tears, I thought.

We had tea and chocolate chip cookies. Rita asked how my mother was doing. My grandmother said, "Fine" and looked away. She talked about the soap operas that they watched. My grandmother loved Erica from *All My Children*. Said she was a woman who knew how to get what she wanted. Rita said she thought Erica was a bitch.

When we were home, listening to talk radio in the living room, I asked my grandmother if she believed in miracles, like the ones she talked about with Margie.

"Sure, sure," she said, not looking up. She was taking the jewelry out of her bag and examining it in the light. I saw bits of dust in the sunlight streaming through the bay window.

"You're not listening to me, Nana."

She put the jewelry back in her handbag and stared at me. "Of course I am."

"Do you think I'll have a miracle and be cured of leukemia?"

"Aiden." She laughed. "You haven't got leukemia. You're as healthy as a horse, silly."

"But you told everybody I was sick."

"Sweetheart, that was to evoke pity."

"What do you mean?"

She spoke hesitantly, like she was a bit ashamed. "Make people feel bad so we can get things from them. I need money to take care of you, Aiden. I'm broke. Your grandfather left me with nothing, and I need to pay for Laura's medical expenses. If Margie notices her jewelry gone, maybe she'll think you took it to help your Nana. I told her I was having a problem paying your hospital bills."

"Sorta like a tribulation, right?"

"Exactly, sweetheart."

"Is my mother a tribulation?"

This time my grandmother's tears were real. They gushed like water from that rock in the Middle East. I knelt before her and put my head in her lap. She rubbed my head and looked out the window. It seemed the tears would never stop.

"Don't worry, Nana. I believe in miracles too. Someday Mom will come home."

And we stayed like that until the sunbeams dimmed and the dust disappeared and her tears stopped.

In the quiet of the room, she whispered, "Keep calm and carry on" to me or to herself. Or to both of us.

Chapter Two

I slept in what had been my mother's room. I hated how girly it looked and had asked my grandmother if we could redecorate. "When we get enough money," she would always say.

That night, as often happened, I awoke to the sound of my grandfather's voice.

Whenever he visited, the bedroom glowed with tiny white lights, illuminated bubbles floating in the air. My face and ears became hot and red, and I heard a buzzing noise. I had confided to my mother about his visits but no one else. Her claim of hearing the voices of dead people led to the diagnosis of schizophrenia. My grandmother and father had her declared mentally incompetent, and she was committed to a psychiatric hospital for treatment. Nana was granted guardianship of her and me until she was well. My brother, Martin, went to live with Aunt Clara, Dad's sister.

"I'm not happy with you, Aiden," my grandfather said. "Why did you allow your grandmother to steal that chalice from the church? 'Tis an awful thing to do."

He sat at the foot of my bed. He wore black bottle-thick glasses, his dark hair a curly mess.

"'Goodness is the only investment that never fails.' A smart man by the name of Toreau said that. You must return the chalice to the church."

"Who's Toorow?"

"A writer. You'll learn about him in school. Mr. Toreau lived about a half hour away from where you do, in Concord."

My grandfather was an autodidact. He never went to college. Couldn't afford it, and he wasn't allowed because of prejudice against Irish immigrants. He and my grandmother, though they did not know each other, emigrated from different parts of Ireland in the late 1930s. When they first arrived, it was difficult for them to get jobs. People hated the Irish. He dug graves during the day and hauled large bags of mail onto the trains at South Station at night. When she was young, my grandmother was a maid for the rich protestant Brahmans on Beacon Hill. Eventually, attitudes changed, she was able to become a licensed practical nurse, and my grandfather—well, he died.

"Aiden, your mind is wandering. You need to listen to me."

"Yes, Grandpa."

"You must get your mother out of McCall's." McCall Hospital is the largest psychiatric hospital in the Boston area. "She needs to live a normal life. And you boys must be with her. Every child should be with his ma. That shower of savages at the hospital are pumping her up with all sorts of terrible medicines." His voice cracked. "Like you, she has the gift, and it is horrible that she is being punished for it."

To me, "second sight" was a curse, a burden.

"It's not a curse, Aiden," my grandfather said, reading my mind. "Second sight has been in your family for years."

"If two people have second sight, do they always see the same spirits?"

"Sometimes, but not always . . . Your grandmother's ma had the gift, and she, too, was demonized. Many believed her, but still, there were those who were cruel. And it only takes a few mean people to ruin the reputation of another."

"What do you mean, *demonized*?"

"Treated badly. Laughed at . . . A mean thing to do to another human being. People said she was tick."

"What do you mean, *tick*?"

"Stupid. Now don't you be an eejit. Follow along. Even your grandmother thought her ma was out of her head. The story goes that your great-grandmother retreated into herself. Once, she was joyful, full of life, but slowly, she withdrew."

"What happened to her?"

"You're not listening, boy, and you ask a lot of questions. A horse startled her, and she fell into a well. Tumbled right over the stone wall, she did. On the night before, she heard banshees calling out to her."

"What's a banshee?"

"A type of fairy or spirit. Her entire family heard the wailing. And there were three knocks on the door, which means someone is going to die. The next day she was bloody dead, her body covered in green muck. All for a bucket of water."

"Didn't they believe her then?"

He laughed, somewhat bitterly. "Of course, Aiden. But what good did it do the poor woman? Dead, she was . . . Son, most people are afraid to believe in things they cannot see. It frightens them, and they become nasty. This is why you must keep your secret for now. Think of a way to free your ma. I don't want Laura to suffer in that awful place."

"What am I supposed to do?"

"You'll figure it out. Your brother will help you."

"Grandpa?" I called a few more times, but the bubbles of light faded, and he was gone. I went to the bathroom and positioned my face under the faucet to drink some water. In the mirror, my face appeared sunburned. The color would fade by the morning as it always did.

I woke to sunlight streaming through lace curtains. The pink wallpaper with vertical lines of tiny roses glowed. The smell of bacon and eggs made my stomach grumble. The digital clock read 9:00 a.m.

I washed my face, checking to see that it had returned to its normal color. Once, the color lingered, and my grandmother thought I had the flu. She made me stay home from school.

Old book smell permeated the air when I passed my grandfather's study. My grandparents had bought this big old house in West Roxbury, an Irish Catholic enclave of Boston, many years before. They had dreams of filling its five bedrooms with children, but that was not to be. Grandpa died young.

Nana's back faced me when I entered the kitchen. On the table was a plate with a white napkin and silverware.

"It's about time you woke up, sleepyhead." She smiled and brought a red mug of coffee to the table, then opened the refrigerator and passed me the cream before moving back to the stove.

"Over hard, as you like them." She flipped an egg and wiped some grease off her pink nightgown. Rollers dangled atop her forehead.

"Thanks, Nana . . . I was thinking."

"Here we go." She laughed. The bacon sizzled.

"Maybe we should return the jewelry to Margie."

"Hand me your plate."

She put two eggs and three strips of bacon on it. The toaster popped.

"Grab the bread, and butter it while it's hot."

She poured herself a cup of coffee—black—sat down, and watched me. Nana rarely ate breakfast. She preferred to smoke and drink coffee, sometimes with whiskey in it. She lit a cigarette and blew a smoke ring.

"Now why would we do that?"

I put three sugars and cream in my coffee, looking down while I stirred. "Because it's wrong to steal."

She laughed. "Phooey." She waved her hand. "Margie doesn't need that jewelry. You see what she wears—that ugly blue sweater. Never changes her clothes. She doesn't go out." She put her cigarette on the ashtray. "I need to sell that jewelry at a pawnshop so I can invest the money in a college fund for your education."

"'Goodness is the only investment that never fails.'"

Her face blanched, and her hazel eyes widened. "Where did you learn that?" She looked behind her as if someone might be there.

"I read it in one of Grandpa's books. It was underlined."

Her face relaxed, and she spoke softly: "I can't tell you the number of times I heard your grandfather say that. And a bunch of other malarkey." She laughed. "He had another favorite expression." She placed her hands on her hips and tilted her head. "'If it was raining soup, the Irish would go out with forks.'"

"That's funny. Why do you tell so many stories? Rita too. And Mom. Always quoting the Bible and writers. It's annoying."

"Part of Irish culture. In the old days, there wasn't much to do in the countryside. We didn't have all the things you kiddos have today. Poor farmers, we were. To entertain ourselves, we read whatever we could, and we made things up. Oh, how we were forced to memorize verse." She gazed blankly and traced a finger along her bottom lip.

"Margie's Irish, and she doesn't quote like you guys."

"Margie was born in America and raised by parents who had money. Your grandfather and I didn't have a pot to pee in. We came from poor folk. Dirt poor. Literally, dirt floors. Our fun was imagination. Margie had *things*. But sometimes imagination is more wonderful than reality." She took my plate and silverware to the sink.

"Are we gonna return the jewelry?"

"How your mind jumps around." She laughed.

"I think what we did is wrong."

"Sometimes you have to spread the wealth. What we did was a venial sin, not a mortal one."

"What's a venial sin?"

"A minor sin. Like a white lie."

"Lying is wrong too."

She turned the faucet on and looked out the window. "Everybody lies, Aiden. Get used to it. The sooner, the better." She rinsed the plates. "Looks like it's going to be a beautiful day."

The blue sky beyond the oak trees was filled with cumulus clouds, a foamy ocean above us. "What's a mortal sin?"

"It's more serious, a grave violation of God's law."

"Was stealing the chalice a venial or mortal sin? And how do you know the difference?"

She turned toward me. "Jesus, Mary, and Joseph. Be more like your brother, Martin. Don't ponder things so much." At times, like my grandfather's, her *th* sounded like *t* or *d*. "Go get ready. We've got Sunday Mass to attend, then we're picking up Martin for dinner and a visit to your mother . . . Scoot." She brushed me away.

I left the kitchen but paused at the bottom of the stairwell to peek at her from beyond the doorframe. She was standing still, gazing out the window, no running water from the faucet, no movement of hands in the sudsy rubber bin. Sometimes I knew what people thought but mostly the thoughts of strangers. The closer your relationship to me, the harder it was for me to read your mind. Later in life, a psychic told me that reading loved ones is difficult because our emotional ties get in the way. This is not always the case. Sometimes a loved one's thought or a vision of the future jolted my brain like electricity.

We went to the ten o'clock Mass at Saint Theresa's, then drove to get Martin on LaGrange Street around the corner, where he lived with my Aunt Clara, Uncle Stanley, and their two children, Greta and Cary. After their separation, my parents felt it was important that Martin and I eat Sunday dinner at Nana's house. They wanted us to remain close, even though it was best financially for us to live in different households. My father helped with money, but he wasn't "good at the parent thing," he said. He lived alone.

Nana pulled in front of the three-decker gray house and honked. Martin waved from the window of the second-floor apartment.

Nana stooped over my lap to look. "Did he come to the window?"

"Yes."

"I don't know why she has to take him to that cult all the way across the city when they live a block away from Saint Theresa's."

"Martin says Aunt Clarise thinks Saint Theresa's is too Catholic."

She snickered. "For Christ's sake. He's Catholic. She's bonkers."

"She hates the pope."

My grandmother frowned. "Why in God's name would she hate the pope?"

"She says he might be the Antichrist. Aunt Clarise thinks that people should be able to ask Jesus directly for forgiveness, instead of going to a priest."

"The Antichrist! That's a horrible thing to say. Why do you keep calling her Clarise? Her name is Clara."

She looked toward the house. "Here he is."

I turned.

He wore a scally cap, dark brown pants, and an army fatigue shirt, smiling as always. How I loved that smile, the space between his teeth, his pointy nose. I slid over when he opened the door.

"How are you, pal?" He messed my hair.

"I'm good. I miss you."

"You're stuck with me for a few hours." He laughed. "And I'm glad to get away from Aunt Clarise. She can be a pain in the ass."

"Watch your language," my grandmother said. "'Clarise, Clarise.' Stop calling her that." She looked to her left and pulled onto the road.

Martin said, "She thinks it sounds prettier than Clara. *Clara* reminds her of that weirdo aunt on *Bewitched*." He shrugged and laughed. His face reddened. "Whatever floats your boat." We all laughed.

As we drove up Centre Street, Nana said, "What did you do at that church today?" She looked in the rearview mirror.

Martin dug into his pants pocket and took out a baggie with pins of birds.

"Talked about pelicans and being good Christian soldiers." He held up the pins.

"And what are you to do with those ugly things?"

"Sell them to raise money for our church." He waved to his friend Dan on the sidewalk. "Well, it's not really a church."

"What do you mean, it's not really a church?"

"It's in a building at a beat-up mall. Used to be a Kmart. Next to a liquor store and a McDonald's."

"Glory be to God. She brings you to a Kmart to worship and receive communion. I'm going to talk to Brian about this." Brian was our father. She shook her head.

Martin and I tried not to laugh. He pinched my leg.

Attempting to get a rise out of her, he added, "We don't receive communion, Nana. We hug one another and make bird sounds."

"Stop your blarney." She turned to look at us. We sailed through a red light.

"Nana, you drove through another red light," I said.

"What's the point of sitting there if no one is coming the other way?"

"That makes sense." Martin elbowed me.

"Now tell me the truth, Martin. You do receive the sacrament, don't you?"

"I *am* telling the truth, Nana. We don't. These people don't believe in it. We hug each other and make bird sounds."

"Bird sounds? This is getting more daft by the second. What do you mean, bird sounds?" She half turned to look at him.

"Ah uh! Ah uh! Ah uh! Real high pitched. That's the sound that pelicans make."

"Why a pelican?" Past CVS, we turned right onto Nana's street.

"A pelican is a symbol of Jesus. Aunt Clarise said a mother pelican will wound herself, striking her breast with her beak to feed the babies with her blood. Like how Jesus gave his life and blood for us."

"Jesus was not a pelican! That's *divvy*. Such foolishness."

"Imagine if we worshiped a pelican nailed to the cross," Martin said.

I laughed.

"Stop that, boys. It's blasphemy to talk that way about our savior. For the love of God!" Nana waved to Mrs. Heffernan, who was clipping flowers in her front yard. "What was that sound again?"

"Ah uh! Ah uh! Ah uh!"

Nana pulled into the driveway and laughed. "Ah uh! Ah uh! Ah uh!" She coughed and patted her chest. "Your Aunt Clara has a bird brain." She put the car in park, and we opened our doors. "Stay outside and enjoy the sun while I go inside and make you a nice dinner."

"What are we having?" I asked.

"Two ducks and a fat hen! And you're going to like it," she said. Which was my grandmother's way of saying, "You'll eat what I serve you, and you'll thank God for the food on your table."

"How 'bout a roast pelican?" Martin said.

"You're fresh," she said, laughing again. "Run ahead." She took her glasses off and wiped them. "After dinner, we're going to visit your mother."

Martin and I climbed the ladder to the treehouse, our leafy island. He and I had built it the year before with help from his friends.

The fort had three levels. I loved sitting on the highest floor most, feeling like the monarch of all that I surveyed—the homes of the Burkes, the Moynihans, the McCarthys, and the O'Sullivans; Rutledge and Oriole Streets in the distance; all the oak, maple, and elm trees planted on middle-class quarter lots where kids played and dogs barked.

The encircling leaves seemed limitless. Those in the sunlight were shiny and warm; those in the shade were cool and soft, like silk. Wind rustled leaves and the tree beneath me swayed. I was sailing on a billowing sea; this treehouse was my ship. I loved the sound of wind, the spirited movement of leaves—breezes passing through distant trees, finally cresting over me like invigorating waves.

We sat on the top floor with our legs folded beneath us. For a moment we were quiet, the both of us looking around. Sunshine dappled the leaves, and a beam of light illuminated Martin's blue eyes. I wanted to tell him something.

He grinned. "Do I have something on my face?" He wiped his nose and forehead.

"I was watching the way light hits your eyes."

"You're like Mom. Always noticing the little things."

I broke a twig off a branch and rubbed it into a leaf on the floor.

"You seem preoccupied, Aiden. Is something bothering you?"

How do you tell a brother you're gay?

"I . . ."

"Spit it out." His smile faded. "You worried about Mom?"

Martin wouldn't have cared about my sexuality. I feared saying the words out loud. Words make thoughts more definite. I hoped I would change. "I was thinking how the green in this leaf reminds me of Nana's descriptions of Ireland."

He looked at the indentations I had made in the waxy outer layer. "Different shades," he said, examining it with his finger. "I want to go to Ireland someday. See where Grandpa came from. Don't you?"

"I want to go everywhere," I said. Someday I would live in a place where I could express my feelings.

His eyebrows rose. "The two of us. We'll visit Grandpa's village on Achill Island."

"I would love to go with you."

"Let's shake on it." He extended his hand. "Promise?"

I promised, and we shook.

We talked about our parents' separation and the events leading up to it.

"Do you think Mom will get better?" Martin's eyes looked solemn. "You're always reading. I bet you know about schizophrenia."

"Maybe she isn't sick."

"What do you mean?"

The wind blew, and one of the branches tapped the floor beneath us.

"Maybe those visions she was having were true."

"Aiden, she was acting crazy. And I can't understand why she would cry for a ghost of an old man. You think she really saw this ghost?"

"Who knows?" I looked down and pulled my legs closer.

"You don't believe in ghosts, do you?"

"I think there are mysteries we can't understand."

He laughed. "You read too many books on ESP and that supernatural junk."

In those days I wanted to tell people that I, too, had visions, but my mother forbade me. "You'll wind up in a place like this," she whispered on one of our visits. "Be patient. They don't understand. God has a plan for all of us."

"The way she harassed the former owners of our house about the old man was psycho. Calling them on the phone, even showing up at their door. Asked them if they knew who the guy was and why he was so sad."

I blushed. "She wanted to help him. Remember how she cried for him."

"She was obsessed, acting like a lunatic. Those people threatened to call the cops."

I was quiet.

"Hey." He touched my arm. "I love Mom. I just want her to get better."

"Let's help her escape."

"Are you crazy? How can we do that? And why would we? She needs to get well."

"I don't think Grandpa would want her locked up in that place," I said. "You've seen the other patients. Mom isn't like them. She seems normal."

"Boys, come in," Nana yelled from the back steps. "Dinner is almost ready, and I want you to wash up and make yourselves presentable."

"Presentable to who?" Martin yelled, rolling his eyes.

"Stop your nonsense, you little *divil*."

Martin started to climb down. I tapped his head.

"I promised you I would go to Ireland. Will you at least consider what I'm saying? When we visit today, decide if you think she belongs there. Promise me that."

"Of course." He punched my leg. "Let's go eat. I'm starving."

We had roast beef as usual. Turnip, green beans, mashed potatoes, and rich, dark gravy. We sat in the wainscoted dining room with floral-patterned wallpaper: greenery interlaced with yellow flowers— my mother called the design "impressionistic."

"You're always so fascinated by the wallpaper, Aiden." Nana looked at it too. "What do you see in there, darling?"

"Beauty."

Martin laughed. "Pass the roast beef. *That* looks beautiful to me."

"Hold your britches, young man. We haven't said grace. Now which one of you will have the honor?" She looked at each of us.

"Let Aiden. He's a better speaker than me."

My grandmother nodded to me, and we all bowed our heads.

"Bless us, oh Lord, and these thy gifts which we are about to receive from thy bounty, through Christ, our Lord. Amen."

"Amen," we all said.

Nana passed the serving plates around. I loved Nana's gravy and poured it over everything. My grandmother relished salt and pepper. Whenever she seasoned her food, Martin and I would count the seconds.

"What are you boys looking at? Eat up. Your dinner will get cold." She motioned to our plates.

Our forks and knives clinked against the plates, a bird chirped outside, and the father of the kids next door hollered, "Get your ass in here, Melissa."

Nana stared at Martin's shirt and said, "Why in God's name are you wearing army fatigues? Doesn't Herself know how to dress you?"

"Aunt Clarise says I need to wear this thing to service." He pulled at the shirt. "I kinda like it. Reminds me of G.I. Joe."

"What do you mean, service?" She placed her hands on the table.

"That church place she takes us."

"Does *she* wear an army shirt as well? And the rest of the lot?"

"We all do. Uncle Stanley, Greta, and Cary. They say we're part of God's army."

Nana spit up a piece of meat, then wiped her yellow dress with a cloth napkin. "What blarney! Those poor kids. Names like that." She held her fork in the air. "Do you two know where she came up with those names?"

"No," Martin said. I shook my head.

"After famous actors. Greta Garbo and Cary Grant."

We both drew blank faces.

She took another sip of her whiskey. "You wouldn't know them. Before your time . . ." She cut another piece of meat and looked at the wallpaper. "They remind me of the gorse shrubs in Ireland. The flowers, I mean. That was a long time ago." She sighed.

Martin and I looked at each other. We wondered how much she'd drunk while she was cooking dinner. Her words slurred. She took another sip. "'There are several good reasons for drinking, and one has just entered my head. If a man can't drink when he's living, then how the heck can he drink when he's dead.' That's what your grandfather used to say." She smiled and looked down. "Oh, that he were with us today." She leaned forward. "Your grandfather would be so proud of the two of you. Look at you. Such good boys and you always will be. I know that." She nodded. "No matter what happens." She lit a cigarette.

"Martin, grab me an ashtray from the kitchen. And make some coffee."

When he left, she said, "Aiden, what do you see?"

"Where?"

"Never you mind. Your grandmother's a bit pissed." She laughed and drank some more. "The coffee will sober me up."

"Are you mad at me?"

"Of course not, sweetheart. *Pissed* is an Irish expression for drunk . . . You're different from other people. Something about you." Martin returned, and she tamped her cigarette. "You're special."

"Thanks," Martin said. "The coffee's brewing."

Nana winked at me, and we all cleared the table.

Chapter Three

The drive to McCall Hospital took a half hour. Located in Somerville, outside Boston proper, you reached the entrance after winding up a slope of lawn to a sandstone admissions building. Beyond that structure and throughout the large campus were several brick edifices with classical flourishes, such as gabled roofs, Roman columns, and ivy-covered walls. Large oak and birch trees, like sentinels, lined the knolls where dormitories from a bygone era stood, rooted in stability, a quality the clinicians nurtured in their patients. We knew the place well. Nana drove the circuitous road to my mother's building, a ward of approximately twenty-five patients, all with a variety of illnesses: schizophrenia, mania, depression, obsessive-compulsive disorder, and borderline personality.

Inside the doorway on the left was the nurses' station and, across from there, the patient lounge with an old television, a scratched pool table, and shelves of tattered books and games. My mother's room was at the end of the hall, a coveted spot. Nana would complain that the hospital costs were outrageous.

I never understood why she was so worried about finances in those days; she worked as a licensed practical nurse at the Massachusetts General Hospital, my father had a good-paying job for the transit authority, and her house was completely paid for. Over the years, I realized that her monetary insecurity was a result of her impoverished beginnings. She often told stories about her struggles in Ireland and "the Troubles." The Irish have an abiding sense of tragedy, the sense that a disaster is just around the corner and what *could* go wrong *would* go wrong. "If you're not fishing, you should be mending your nets," she would say.

"Can I help you?" A short, small-framed nurse with bleached hair and blue eye shadow greeted us.

"We're here to visit my daughter, Laura Glencar." My grandmother motioned to us. "These are her sons, Martin and Aiden." She puckered her lips. "I don't think I've met you. Are you new?"

"I started last week. My name is Nancy. You can call me Nurse Nancy. Let me find out who's taking care of your daughter today. Dora Fender, you said?" She turned to look at the dry-erase board with patient names, room numbers, and nursing assignments.

"Laura Glencar!" Nana rolled her eyes at us. "This one's a tool," she mumbled.

"She's new, Nana," I whispered.

"She's not new to hearing," she whispered back, then smiled at the nurse.

"It's me!" Nurse Nancy said.

"What did I tell you?" Nana said to us, a little too loudly.

"Right this way." Nurse Nancy's hips swiveled in front of us.

"We know how to get there, Nancy Nurse. You don't have to bring us. Your time would be better spent memorizing that board, don't you think?" Nana smiled at her.

"But it's policy."

"Must be a new policy. Never happened before."

Nurse Nancy fingered her necklace. "I want to do things right."

"I can understand, dear," my grandmother said.

"You have some lovely visitors," Nurse Nancy announced to my mother, who was seated by the window looking at patients walking across the lawn. She turned and smiled gloriously, as she always did. My mother was an attractive woman, at that time thirty-three years old—wavy auburn hair, light green eyes with specks of gold, and fair skin with a sprinkle of tiny freckles on her cheeks.

"Give me a hug." She extended her arms. My grandmother sat on the bed next to her and plopped her handbag near the pillow. Martin and I embraced her. I can still smell traces of her Avon perfume all these years later. I will never forget that scent.

"Thank you, Nancy. You made my day."

Nancy beamed and left.

"She's a dumb girl," Nana said. "Didn't even know you were her patient for the day. Can you imagine that?"

"Ma, don't be so hard on her. She just started."

"Yes, she told us that. I think it's a poor excuse. But never mind." She looked at us boys. "Martin, why don't you go to the patient lounge and play pool for a bit?" She looked at me. "You too. I want to speak with your mother alone."

"Aiden hates pool, Ma. Let him stay."

"I'll go. I want to investigate," Martin said, winking at me. My mother's eyes narrowed as she looked at us.

He ran out of the room.

"Slow down," my mother called after him.

"Aiden and I have something for you," said Nana.

My mother clapped her hands and smiled. Outside the window, patients walked back and forth, arms behind them, not talking with one another, lost in thought, some muttering to themselves or moving their hands in bizarre ways.

Nana reached into her handbag and carefully placed three items on the blue bedspread: the gold necklace and cross; a small jar of red wine; and, finally, the golden chalice, which sparkled in the well-lit room.

"Mom, where did you get that cup?" My mother's eyes widened. "It looks like part of the queen's crown jewels." She laughed.

"A friend of mine loaned it to me." Nana warned me with her eyes.

"Who?" My mother giggled and raised the chalice. "Such beautiful stones. This must be worth a fortune. Do you know a museum curator?"

"You could call Joshua that. He works for a very reputable institution. Started it from the ground up. The building is as grand as a temple."

"Where is it?" My mother's eyebrows squished together.

"Somewhere in the midsection of east Texas."

"Texas?" My mother laughed. "I didn't know you knew anyone from Texas." She cupped her palms over the chalice in her lap.

"You don't know everything about me."

"I think you're telling me a fib." My mother laughed, and her shoulders drooped. "It's beautiful, but what am I supposed to do with it?"

"Drink this wine."

She kissed my grandmother's cheek. "It's gorgeous. Thank you."

"I have to return it, Laura."

"I figured that."

"So you'll drink wine from the chalice?"

"What is this all about?" My mother looked from my grandmother to me.

"Joshua says it has healing powers."

"There's nothing wrong with me." She folded her arms. "But if it will make you happy, I'll drink the wine. Pour some, but be careful not to stain the bed."

As my mother sipped, Nurse Nancy came in.

"I'm sorry to bother you, but your boy has started quite a commotion in the patient lounge. He's giving bird pins to everyone. The patients are making queer sounds."

"Ah uh! Ah uh! Ah uh!" my grandmother said.

"Yes, that's it."

"It's the sound of a pelican. A symbol of Christ." My grandmother crossed herself as in church.

"A pelican?" My mother looked at me with wrinkled brows.

"Martin learned it from Aunt Clarise's church," I replied.

"I'm sorry, Nancy. Tell Martin to come back here. He means no harm."

"Hey. What are you drinking?" Nurse Nancy looked at the small jar of wine, which my grandmother was quickly shoving into her handbag.

"Cranberry juice. It prevents urinary tract infections," Nana said.

Nurse Nancy put her hands on her hips. "I hope that's all it is. Laura is on medication, and alcohol could interact with her meds in a negative way."

"Of course it's not alcohol," Nana said. "I'm a Christian woman. Today is Sunday. In our family, we abstain from alcohol in reverence to our Lord Jesus Christ. I'm offended that you would suggest such a thing, Nancy Nurse."

"It's Nurse Nancy. . . Maybe this son"—she looked at me—"could bring his brother back to the room?"

"His name's Aiden." My grandmother smiled. "But you're not good with names, are, you dear?" She put the chalice back in her handbag, then wrapped the gold necklace and cross around my mother's neck. "Don't feel bad; we all have our weaknesses. Don't we, Aiden?"

"Yes, Nana."

My mother was grinning, trying to suppress laughter. She had a boisterous laugh, and I knew her stomach must have hurt from holding back.

I found Martin surrounded by several patients flapping their arms like wings, chirping: "Ah uh! Ah uh! Ah uh!"

Martin was laughing so hard that he didn't notice me standing behind him. "That's it. You're a pelican flying across the ocean in search of your loved ones. Someday you'll be home with them," he told the crowd.

"Martin!"

"What?" He turned around.

"You've got to come back to the room. The nurse is mad."

"The nurse is mad! The nurse is mad!" the patients repeated.

One old lady with cropped red hair and a long, thin nose said, "There's always a party pooper." She glared at me.

Nancy appeared in the doorway. "Relax. Take deep breaths," she said to the patients. She moved her arms downward a few times.

"Settle down! Settle down! Take deep breaths. Take deep breaths," they answered.

Martin and I escaped, laughing as we ran down the hallway.

"These people are crazy. I feel bad for them. And you're right, Mom doesn't compare, but I'm still not convinced she should leave yet."

I was disappointed, but I was determined to convince him. One of my qualities is persistence.

We entered the room out of breath. Martin told what happened as only he could do.

When he had finished, my mother said, "Those patients are too impressionable. You caused headaches for the nurses. Be more considerate."

"Sorry, Mom."

"I think you should apologize to the nurses before you leave."

"I will."

Nana said, "Aunt Clara bears some responsibility for this hullabaloo."

"How so?"

"Tell your ma about Herself and that daft fundraiser for the cult." Nana shook her head in disgust.

Martin explained the meaning of the pelicans and again imitated their sound. Before long, we all were laughing.

"Ah uh! Ah uh! Ah uh!" my grandmother squawked.

Even my mother joined in.

As I recall that scene at McCall's, I smile. How Martin eased my sense of loneliness in those years. My family was happy. Creating joy was his passion.

When we returned to Nana's place, she called Aunt Clara. Martin and I sat at the kitchen table while she turned her back to us, dangling the long phone cord in her hand.

"Hello, Clara . . . I'm sorry. Yes, Clarise. Dear, I was wondering if Martin could spend the night. The boys need time together, and the two of them are so exhausted. They were reprimanded for the bird pins at the hospital. It really was quite embarrassing. Shook them up terribly." She winked at both of us. "Martin is asleep on the couch, and Aiden is in his room, probably knackered as well."

She rolled her eyes and twisted the cord. "Yes, yes. I know Martin's your responsibility." Nana motioned for one of us to pour her a whiskey sour. We knew the drill. Martin went to the living room bar; I pushed the ashtray toward her and removed a Parliament cigarette from her handbag. I used her Bic lighter and took a puff, then passed it to her. Martin returned with her drink. Nana inhaled the cigarette deeply while she listened to Aunt Clara on the other end of the phone. Clara had an annoying high-pitched voice. I could hear it from where I sat. Nana opened and closed her hand repeatedly while Clara yapped on.

"Yes, I understand what the judge determined . . . Clara—I mean, Clarise." Her lips tightened and her eyes rolled as she held back a laugh. "Dear, I'm sure you will not get in trouble."

Nana gulped her drink and turned away from us, mumbling something into the phone. Then we heard her say, "Brilliant. Yes. You're a sweet woman. Thank you for considering the boys, especially after the upset with those pelican pins. The nurse was quite angry. They need time to bond and recover. Wouldn't you agree, love?

"What an arse!" she said after hanging up. She puffed her cigarette. "What ya looking at?"

We were both laughing.

"Go to Aiden's room and get ready for bed. The both of you."

"It's only nine," Martin said.

"It's past midnight somewhere, so it's late. Now shoo!" She waved her hands. "I'll be up in a half hour or so to say your prayers. Until then, you can listen to the stereo."

When we were in the bedroom, Martin said, "I don't blame you for hating this room. It looks like a girl's." He picked up a doll from my mother's dresser. "You can get rid of some of this stuff. Put the dolls and teddy bears in the closet."

"I don't want to touch Mom's things. It feels wrong."

"I guess I know what you mean." He spied the telescope by the window. "I forgot all about that thing. Let's look at the stars."

I took my Doors album *Other Voices* out of its paper sleeve, placed in on the stereo turntable, and moved the needle to my favorite track. The lyrics of "Ships w/Sails" played as I met Martin by the window. He was bent over, adjusting the aim of the telescope, peering at the night sky.

"Aiden." He pointed. "Some of those stars are dead now. It takes the light that long to get here. I think that's amazing." The Doors' keyboardist Ray Manzarek sang, comparing his love to sails and their love for the ocean wind. Would he be thinking of someone again? he continued. Would he ever pass this way again? Someday he would return, he said. We all return, I thought.

Nana entered the room with folded sheets, which she placed at the bottom of my bed. "Such awful music. It's time for prayer." She placed her hands on her ears while I turned off the stereo.

The three of us knelt by the window and looked toward the dark vault of shimmering sky. A bright star gleamed above the crescent moon. I imagined it was journeying to someplace beyond.

"Isn't God's design magnificent? When I was a child, I would stand in the meadow, hoping to see a shooting star."

"Did you see any?" I said.

"Lots of them. They were spectacular . . . I want to tell you something important. Someday I will die, and you must remember what I say to you now."

"You're not dying for ages."

"Don't interrupt me, Martin. Hold this in your heart: the most important thing in the world is family. You must always look out for one another, and your mother too. No matter where you end up, communicate with one another, keep in touch. Family is always first. Promise me that."

We did.

Family is important, I thought, and it should be. But how intimate were any of us? Were Martin and I close? In some ways, we were. We did things together. We talked about external things in a cursory way—girls, friends, school, and the events within our home life. But we rarely exposed what was in our hearts—our longings, our fears, and our doubts. Intimacy in an Irish Catholic household is taboo. Knowledge about family members is limited, secrets are guarded, subjects are avoided, but love is always strong.

I remembered the promises that Martin and I made earlier, and it struck me that without promises, all of us are lost souls. Promises are the sails that guide us. They move us toward our destinies.

"Now bend your heads and touch your hands." She placed her hand on Martin's head, gently pushing it downward. I caught him smiling at me when he opened an eye.

We joined her as she began: "There are four corners on my bed. There are four angels at my head. Matthew, Mark, Luke, and John, God bless the bed I sleep upon. Amen."

Nana stood up. "Now get your arses into bed." She pulled a cot out of the closet. "One of you can sleep here. I'll put the sheets on." I helped her. Martin found a pillow in the closet.

"Aiden, you can have the bed."

When Nana left and the lights were out, I said, "What you said about the light from the stars. Are you sure that's true?"

"What part?"

"That some of those stars are dead now."

"Yeah. I read it in *Scientific American*. You're not the only brainiac in this family. I think a lot." He laughed.

"Do you know how something can be dead and alive at the same time?" I said.

"Not really. But it sounds cool." He laughed. "Go to sleep, brother. I love you."

"Love you too."

Chapter Four

The next day, we drove Martin to Aunt Clara's house. When we were in front, Nana beeped the horn. "Let her come out. I'm older than Herself."

"I'll go in, Nana," Martin said.

"Hold on. I want to speak with her. I don't like that church she has you going to."

Martin and I eyed one another. When Nana had something to say, she never held back. At the front door, Aunt Clara, her hair in a bun, cupped the heads of Greta and Cary at her side. She smiled and waved.

Nana reached over me and rolled down the window. "Please come here," she called.

Aunt Clara frowned. "What is it?"

"I want to talk with you. Come to the car!"

Aunt Clara whispered something to the children, and they disappeared into the room behind her. She teetered on high heels as she walked toward us and circled the car to Nana's open window.

"What in the hell type of church are you bringing Martin to?"

Aunt Clara grimaced and spoke slowly. "It's a nondenominational Christian church. The people are very kind." She placed her hand on the door and stuck her head in.

"Hi," Martin said. I waved.

Nana said, "PU. That perfume you're wearing stinks." She pinched her nostrils.

Aunt Clara folded her arms and twisted her bottom lip. Her eyes fluttered, and her chin moved forward. "It's Chanel No. 5. Very expensive."

Nana coughed. "I don't care how much it cost. The sales clerk hoodwinked you. Please move away from the car. I might respiratory arrest, and I don't think you know CPR."

Aunt Clara pushed a strand of hair from her forehead. "Actually, I'm certified. And for your information, Chanel is a sign of good taste." She smirked.

"Smells like a funeral parlor. The morticians must buy stock in the company."

"All right, Catherine. I'm tired of your sarcastic attacks. I don't criticize your tacky Sears outfits." Her face reddened.

"There's nothing wrong with Sears, Clara."

"Clarise, please." She banged the door. "Now cut to the chase! Greta and Cary are in there alone." She looked toward the front door.

"That's another thing. You putting on airs with that silly name. I'm not sure I like Martin living with you. Humility is a virtue, and you don't seem to possess it."

I shoved Martin and whispered, "Just go."

"Nana. Everything's cool. I'll get out," he said.

"Hold on," she snapped, turning to look at him. "Take your hand off the door this instant!

"I don't want you taking him to that cult any longer," she continued. "Saint Theresa's is right around the corner. He can go Sundays with Aiden."

Aunt Clara put her hands on her hips and laughed. "Catherine, you're forgetting the judge gave me custody of Martin. If you don't like the way I run my household, take it up in court." She turned, saying over her shoulder, "Come on, Martin. You have chores to do."

As she walked down the brick path, Martin kissed my grandmother and me on our cheeks, then opened the door and ran to catch up with her.

My grandmother yelled, "I hope it doesn't involve cleaning up pelican poop. He could get a disease." Then she said to me, "She's mad as a box of frogs."

"What does that mean?"

"Herself is a crazy bitch." She pulled quickly onto the road, the car screeching. "I'd like to push her down, kick her shin, and poke her eyes out."

I laughed. She looked at me in the rearview mirror and chuckled too.

We ran over a branch and bounced in our seats, laughing harder.

Later that day, I walked to the end of Park Street to the intersection with Centre Street. My father's bus route, Charles River 36, began at Forest Hills in Jamaica Plain and took him through West Roxbury. I would estimate the time of his arrival. My stomach felt queasy. Three other people were waiting for the bus—two older women talking about how times had changed and a businessman sitting on the bench reading the *Globe*.

I was always nervous seeing my father. He was so different from my talky mother. Dad gave short simple answers. Having a conversation was difficult. When I was older, I realized he was an introvert. He spoke to me through actions—money, gifts, and help. Raised in a stoic Irish Catholic household, the oldest of five, he became an adult early, taking on the responsibilities for his siblings when his father died young from a stroke.

The familiar white-and-yellow bus drew close. One of the ladies looked at her watch and said, "You can't rely on the posted schedule."

They both moved toward the curb. The businessman nodded at me, folded his paper, and stood.

The bus came to a halt, and the doors whooshed open. I let the others board first, then climbed the steps and sat on the blue plastic chair to my left. Dad smiled. He wore a light blue shirt with a maroon tie and the circular emblem of the *T* on his right shoulder. After checking his rearview mirror to make sure the passengers were seated, he pulled into the street. The bus was not crowded. Someone had written "Hurry up please, it's time" on the wall across from me. I was glad the people sat farther back so I could have privacy when I talked to my father.

"What's up, Aiden?"

"School starts soon."

"You must be excited." He looked at me quickly, then continued staring forward.

"Yeah."

"You don't *sound* excited." He laughed.

"Dad, I wanted to talk with you about Mom."

"OK. Shoot."

"I think we should get her out of that place."

He looked in the rearview mirror and whispered, "Aiden, your Mom is mentally ill."

"I don't think she is."

"Are you a psychiatrist?"

"No."

"I understand that you want to be with her. Martin too. But I don't think she's well."

I heard a creepy laugh from the back of the bus. A woman in a floral dress with stringy gray hair pointed her finger at me and grinned.

"Who's that lady?"

My father looked in the mirror. "Which one?"

"The lady in the dress with red-and-yellow flowers on it. She's pointing at me."

"I don't see her." He pulled the bus over at the next stop and opened the door. Two girls with lollipops in their mouths got on. They stared at me and giggled. I must have looked frightened. My father glanced at me too. "Are you OK?" Then he moved the bus into the traffic again. "You look pale."

"I'm fine. Just a little stomachache."

"Maybe you have a fever. We're almost at LaGrange Street. Are you getting off there?"

"Yeah, I guess." My routine was to get off there and walk through Billings Field up to Rutledge Street, where I turned right onto Park, then walked a block to Nana's house.

"Have Catherine check your temperature. Fevers sometimes cause people to hallucinate."

"OK."

"Aiden, I love your mom, but she needs to get better."

"Do you think we'll ever be a family again?"

I heard the lady cackling by the rear door of the bus. Again she pointed at me.

"Why do you keep looking back there?"

"I was looking at those girls."

He smiled. "You're too young for girls. Stay away from them. They're a pain in the ass."

"Do you think Mom's a pain in the ass?"

"No. Unique, maybe. Creative, yes. Smart. But a pain in the ass, nah."

When we reached LaGrange, I kissed his cheek and got off. He waved to me and drove on. When I turned to walk up LaGrange, I saw the woman in the floral dress standing by a trash barrel. She spit on the sidewalk and stared at me. Again she smiled. Her gray eyes were milky. She scratched her wrists with long, pale fingernails. I noticed red lines and scabs along her forearms.

I walked quickly, afraid to turn around. The air smelled awful, like sulfur, and I wondered if it was coming from the dumpster behind the Chinese restaurant. I could hear the clicks from her heels. When I came to Billings Field, I stopped. The clicking stopped. I froze. She must have been standing close. I felt her breath on my neck, and she whispered into my ear, "You little faggot." The sulfur smell was her breath.

"And you're an ugly witch," I said and spun around. She was nowhere. For a few moments, I looked up and down the street. A group of boys with a basketball entered the park. Aunt Clara's house was about ten houses away. I didn't see her kids or Martin in the yard, where they sometimes played wiffle ball. I walked toward the alley behind the Chinese restaurant and checked to see if she was hiding behind the dumpster. I wanted to scream at her. A disheveled waiter came out the back door.

"What you doing? Get away from here. No food. Garbage."

"I was looking for my dog."

"No dog here." He threw a bag of trash in the dumpster. "Get outta here before I call police."

I ran into Billings Field, past the basketball court where the boys were playing. My heart raced, and I was out of breath. I bent over and vomited. For ten minutes I lay on the field, waiting for my heart to slow and my stomach to settle.

I got home as Nana pulled into the driveway. I met her by the car.

"You look weak as a kitten!" She shut the door and placed her palm on my forehead. "Aiden, you're all sweaty and a bit warm. Are you sick?"

"No. I was running fast."

She cocked her head. "And why were you running fast?"

"I couldn't wait to see you."

"Such palaver. You're like your grandfather." She laughed, then sniffed and looked at my shirt. "What's that smell?" Her eyes widened. "Is that vomit on your jersey?"

"I threw up."

She grabbed my arm. "Let's get in the house. I want to take your temperature."

She made me sit at the kitchen table while she stuck a thermometer under my tongue.

"I'm fine," I mumbled.

"Don't talk," she snapped, pouring water into a teakettle and placing it on the stove. "What you need is a nice cup of tea."

She took the thermometer out of my mouth, squinted, and said, "Ninety-nine point eight."

"I told you I wasn't sick."

"Don't talk back to your grandmother. You have a slight fever." The kettle whistled, and she poured two cups of tea. She put milk and sugar in my mug.

"Are you upset about something?" She placed her warm hand over mine. "You still feel clammy. What's wrong, darling?"

I could feel my eyes tear up.

"Speak to me."

I wanted to say so much. Tell her I was afraid our family would never be together. Tell her grandpa visited me at night. Tell her I feared people would learn my secrets and that I, too, would be placed in a psychiatric hospital. Tell her I felt so alone, that I wanted to have friends, that I prayed to God every night to make me normal. I wanted to tell her about the horrible old woman who whispered the shame I refused to acknowledge, even when alone.

"I'm going to take a nap."

"It'll do you good."

That night at 12:43 a.m., Grandpa visited. Again the room was illuminated with white bubbles, and my face flushed. He sat farther up the bed, one hand placed on my blanketed leg. I propped my head on the pillows. He seemed more real than before. I could *feel* his hand. His glasses reflected the light that surrounded us.

"Aiden, I need you to listen carefully. I must explain important things."

"I'm listening, Grandpa."

"That woman on your bus—"

"How did you—?"

"Don't interrupt me, son. There are some things you can never understand. Not yet. When you pass over, you will know, but not until then. Trust what I say."

"Yes, Grandpa."

"I think she's a pooka. Even on this side, there are some things we don't know for certain."

"What is that?"

"A pooka is an evil spirit not to be trusted. In Ireland, the rural folk believed that nature was full of spirits who inhabited every place in the natural world—trees, mountains, streams, and wells, for example. If a human disturbs these spaces, the spirits get mad and seek revenge. The dwelling of a pooka is the worst place to unsettle.

This trickster spirit may seek revenge on the family. For generations, even. Be careful of this woman. If she is a pooka, she can change her form into a variety of animals—a cat, a goat, a horse, even an eagle. A shape shifter, the Irish call them. And listen to what she says. Often, pookas relay veiled messages about your future."

"This is so confusing, Grandpa. And scary."

"Of course it's scary, Aiden. But life is full of difficulties and scary things. You must persevere."

"When will I know if she's a pooka?"

"*When* is relative. Remember, time does not exist. Everything is happening all at once. 'Tis our minds that give us the illusion of the stream of events we call life. You already understand, but you don't know you do."

"If everything is happening all at once, am *I* dead now too?"

"You are both dead and alive, a young boy and an old man. All that you experience in your mortal state has already happened and *will* always happen."

I thought of what Martin said about the stars. "That sounds so crazy." I put the pillow over my head.

"Don't dwell on all these things. Live your life. I want you to remember something. Take that pillow off your head and listen."

I sat up.

"It says in Corinthians that 'we are hard pressed on every side, but not crushed; perplexed, but not in despair; persecuted, but not abandoned; struck down, but not destroyed.' No matter what anyone whispers in your ear, remember my whisper first." His voice lowered, and he bent forward. "You are how God meant you to be. And God loves you."

I was embarrassed that my grandfather seemed to know all about me.

"The important thing is to never stop questioning. That is why we live . . .You're going to be a wonderful student. You will even write this conversation in a book."

"How do you know?"

"Look at this block of wood." It appeared atop my shins. "The front represents the future; the middle is the present; and the back part"—he tapped the end—"is the past."

"I don't get it."

"Do you see the entire block?"

"Yes."

"That's life. Eternity. There is no division between the past, present, and future; there is, rather, a single existence. Our brains can't handle everything happening at once. Mad as a box of frogs, we'd be."

I laughed. "Nana said that."

"It's an expression from the old country."

"So you're saying I'm alive in the past and the future, just as I am in the present."

"Yes. But your consciousness is like a small flashlight that can only shine on one part of the block at a time."

"That sounds weird."

"I've got to go, son. But think on this saying: 'The most beautiful experience we can have is the mysterious . . . Whoever does not know it and can no longer wonder, no longer marvel, is as good as dead, and his eyes are dimmed.'"

"I like that, Grandpa."

"I've given you enough to ponder. Keep your eyes open. Life is more mysterious than you could ever imagine. And more beautiful too."

He disappeared. The room was black. I pulled up the blanket and stared into the darkness.

In September of 1976, I started ninth grade at Boston Latin School, the oldest public high school in the country. Martin waited for me at the Centre Street bus stop where my father had picked me up. He wanted me to feel comfortable the first day, so he walked up the hill from LaGrange Street, where he could have hopped on the bus. Both streets intersected with Centre.

Other Latin School students were there; everyone knew and liked Martin. I felt proud that he was my brother. He introduced me to his friends and pulled me to the back of the bus, where we sat in the last row, over the warm rumbling engine.

"Don't be nervous, brother. You're gonna love it." He grinned. "Now me. I'm not so crazy about school, but I know how much you like learning."

The students on the bus teemed with excitement; many hadn't seen each other during the summer months. They were catching up on what they had done during the vacation. The ride was bumpy and jerky with pauses to pick up other students. When the bus stopped, the wheels squealed. I watched the faces of the kids as Martin chatted with his friends. He told jokes and stories, talking loudly, laughing heartily. We had such different personalities. I was the observing, quiet one, who liked to study people and get lost in my thoughts. Martin was the classic extrovert. Periodically, Martin glanced at me and smiled, sometimes putting his hand on my neck as he talked.

A tall woman with wavy blonde hair and blue eyes stood in the aisle beside a girl in a black skirt and green blouse. The girl brushed light brown ringlets of hair off the cheek of her pale oval face. She wasn't talking to anyone, simply staring straight ahead. Sometimes she turned to glance at the street outside, extending her thin body toward the window. The seat next to her was empty. Why didn't the woman sit down?

"Do kids often bring their parents the first day?" I said to Martin, who was telling a story about how he swam through jellyfish at the beach in South Boston. His friend Dan, a tall, handsome guy with short-cropped brown hair and perfect white teeth, said, "You're lucky you didn't get stung."

"I floated like a butterfly so they couldn't sting me like a bee," he said, twisting the words of Muhammad Ali. Then he turned to me. "Not usually. Why?"

I pointed. "That lady in white with the blonde hair and shiny face."

He looked. "I don't see any lady."

"Right there, standing next to the girl with the green blouse and curly hair. About five rows from the front. See?"

He punched my bicep playfully. "Stop messing with me. You know there isn't anyone standing by her."

Dan looked too. "Aiden likes to tell stories as much as you." He laughed. "Guess it runs in the family."

I realized that this was another spirit. As if reading my mind, she looked at me and nodded. The girl she was standing beside was oblivious to her presence. I would ask my grandfather about her. I opened the window and watched the people in their cars. The smell of the exhaust fumes reminded me of the gray-haired lady. I hoped I would never see her again. In about an hour, we were exiting the bus at 78 Avenue Louis Pasteur in Boston.

The large brick building was intimidating. Students rushed toward the grand entrance, where an American flag hung beneath a triangular pediment held up by four Corinthian columns. The building, neoclassical in style, was three storied with several double-hung windows, at least fifteen across; a small cement capstone centered above each of them. PUBLIC LATIN SCHOOL was engraved above the columns.

When we got off the bus, kids shouted Martin's name and ran up to him. I stood halfway between him and the wide cement stairs that led to the front door. Students whizzed by me, laughing and gossiping.

"Wait up," Martin shouted to me, then patted his buddies on their backs before running over.

"Who's that scary-looking guy with the red hair and bulging eyes?" I asked. The guy's face was statue white and flabby. He folded his arms and surveyed the students, like a hawk from the top of a tree.

"That's the headmaster, Mr. Castellanos. He's a real asshole."

As if hearing Martin, he turned in our direction, looking me directly in the eye. His stern face, black jacket, and thick gray tie gave him the appearance of an undertaker. I noticed the students slowed down and walked orderly as they passed him, heads turned to avoid eye contact.

"Hey, Mr. C.," Martin said when we reached the top step.

"Mr. Glencar. Come over here."

"Sure." Martin grinned. "Come on, Aiden," he whispered. "Don't be afraid of him. He tries to act tough, but I think he's a pussy."

Mr. Castellanos stood in front of an arched doorway surrounded by recessed cement columns supporting a large entablature. "This must be Aiden." He looked me up and down. I straightened my light blue shirt self-consciously.

"Yeah," Martin said. "He's the smart one." He laughed.

"Hmm," Mr. Castellanos said, rubbing his right index finger along his cheek. "I've seen his test scores. You're as smart, but you don't apply yourself."

Mr. Castellanos put both hands firmly on my shoulders. "You better do well, young man." Then he glanced at the rush of students around us. "A third of our freshmen don't make it through their first semester. Don't let that happen to you." He said to Martin, "Take good care of your brother, and no trouble from you this year."

"Mr. C., I'm gonna be as straight as an arrow. No more fights."

"We'll see. Run along. Get to your homerooms before the bell."

Chapter Five

In the main hallway, students lined up at tables behind which six faculty members sat with lists of student homeroom assignments. Martin gently pushed me to the line in front of the F–J poster. The hallway smelled of shellac from the mahogany-paneled walls with insets of carved ivy. The occasional smell of cigarettes, perfume, and sweat wafted in the air. At the top of the wall, fluorescent lights illuminated paintings of former headmasters. A large purple-and-white banner depicted a wolf with two suckling cubs, the words SCHOLA LATINA BOSTONIENSIS underneath and COND, followed by Roman numerals. I couldn't hear very well because of the number of students saying their names, and I was distracted by the clicking sound of a large clock.

"Tell her your last name," Martin said.

"Glencar."

"What was that?" The thin-faced woman scratched a mole on her chin.

"Glencar," Martin answered loudly from behind.

She blinked and bit her chapped lip as she traced a finger down the roster.

"Aiden or Martin?"

"Aiden," I said.

"You've got to speak up." She sighed and cupped her ear. "The acoustics in this hall are terrible."

"Aiden," I shouted, more forcefully than I intended.

She handed me a paper. "Room two-oh-six . . . Next."

Once Martin got his room number, which was on the third floor, he brought me to my class. The hallways were lined with blue lockers, many with dents and scratches. Brown-and-black linoleum tiles glistened with new wax. Teachers stood outside their classroom doorways, answering student questions, looking at papers handed to them, and pointing in various directions.

"There's your room," Martin said. "The tall guy with brown hair and glasses. Mr. Rossi. He's a bit high strung, but you'll be able to handle him."

I hesitated, feeling a pang of separation anxiety.

"Aiden, don't worry. It's the first day. Everyone's nervous, especially the freshmen. I'll see you at lunch."

"How will I know where to find you?"

"Don't worry, brother. I'll find *you*." He smiled and dashed off.

"Wait," Mr. Rossi said as I walked into the room.

He pulled on the back of my shirt. "I need your paper."

He looked at it. "Names are written on slips of paper on top of the desks. Students are seated in alphabetical order. Welcome to Boston Latin School."

When the bell rang, most of the desks were filled. Mr. Rossi told us the school rules, but I half listened. I was more interested in my peers. My classmates were of mixed ethnicities from the many neighborhoods in Boston. Students were required to take a test for admission. The first public high school in the United States, Boston Latin was established by the Puritans. The curriculum focused on a classical education that included the study of Latin and ancient Greek. In an era of declining schools, entrance to Boston Latin was prized because of its rigorous curriculum, high ranking, and prestigious history. Some of the distinguished alumni are Cotton Mather, Benjamin Franklin, Samuel Adams, John Hancock, Charles Bullfinch, and Ralph Waldo Emerson.

Mr. Rossi alluded to the famous alumni and told us to look at the students to the left and right of us, echoing what the principal had told me. "One of them will not be here next year."

Some kids sat stiffly in their seats with anxious expressions; a few were taking notes. I supposed those were the ones who would "be here" next year. Others sneered or sat casually, yawning, bored, or tired from the commute and early morning hour.

In the back, one seat from the windows, I noticed the girl from the bus. She caught me staring and looked at the black girl behind her, who whispered something. The blonde lady in white was standing in the aisle. She placed a finger on her lip and pointed with her other hand toward Mr. Rossi, prompting me to turn around.

"You with the blue shirt in the third row. Look at me while I talk. What's your name again?"

"Aiden Glencar, sir."

"Show respect when your teacher is speaking."

A girl laughed somewhere to my right.

"That goes for you, too, young lady," he said. Spikes of purple and green hair rose from her scalp like porcupine quills. When Mr.

Rossi turned from looking in her direction, she stuck her tongue out at me. I fought the urge to turn around and look at the lady, so I pretended to listen to Mr. Rossi while I read the poster quotes above his head. "The life of the dead is placed in the memory of the living"—*Cicero* and "Everything that exists is in a manner the seed of that which will be"—*Marcus Aurelius*.

I thought of my grandfather and his explanation of time. When the bell rang, I turned once more to look at the girl. The woman in white was gone. My first class, I learned from the schedule Mr. Rossi had distributed, was physical education. I looked at the school map that he had given us and turned right to descend the stairwell at the end of the hall.

"You're cute," the girl with the ringlets said. She winked at me and moved quickly forward.

As I approached the gymnasium, I became nervous. I was a terrible athlete, running the wrong way on the football field and forgetting to dribble during basketball. Unlike Martin, I had no athletic prowess. Martin could do everything physical. Tall and sinewy, he was a first-class runner and swimmer. His friends called him Seal because of his agility in the water.

I pushed open one of the blue double doors. The gym smelled of sweat and dirty sneakers mixed with the scent of floor wax. A tall light-skinned black man was calling names from his clipboard and telling kids to line up against a wall with Grade Nine on a makeshift poster. I crossed the shiny yellow wooden floor and stood with my back against the cool cinderblock wall, waiting for my name to be called. The man's voice was gruff, and he kept rubbing the shadow of a beard along the side of his face. Against the opposite wall under a purple-and-white banner with the school name and logo stood the blonde lady, smiling at me and pointing to my left. A few students down, the girl from the bus and homeroom blew bubble gum from her mouth. She rolled her green eyes every time the teacher barked a name and pointed to the end of the line.

"You!" he said. "Take that gum out of your mouth. Throw it in the trash outside the gym door."

The girl laughed, pulled her shoulders back, and walked briskly across the floor.

"Gallagher, Hope," he shouted.

"That's me." She stopped halfway across the gym and turned.

"Hurry up and get rid of that gum. You're next."

"Yes, sir," she said.

"Glencar, Aiden"

I waved.

He looked me up and down, then told me to get in line.

When we were in order against the wall, he began with the rules. I always hated the first day of school because you heard the same things from every teacher: no tardiness, no food or drink, no talking over the teacher, always raise your hand, dress appropriately (in this case, with gym shorts, white T-shirt and socks, sneakers) and other boring guidelines.

"I'm Mr. Hightower," he said.

Hope turned and whispered, "It suits him. Don't you think?"

"What?"

"The name. He's so tall."

"What did I say about talking?" He pointed at Hope. "Step forward."

"Yes, sir."

"Are you going to be a troublemaker?"

"No, sir. I apologize."

The blonde woman across the way had vanished.

"Good. Get back in line." He shook his head and wrote something on his clipboard.

In a short while, we were told that the girls would be playing softball outside, and the boys would be playing basketball. At the far end of the gym, another instructor, a short chubby white guy, put his kids in groups to play volleyball. I spotted Martin.

Soon we were divided into teams, and Mr. Hightower threw the basketball into the air. A tall redhead from my team passed it to me. I moved toward the net, barely dribbling at first, then not bothering to dribble at all. It seemed stupid. The other team members screamed foul. Mr. Hightower blew his whistle and came over to me.

He put his hand on my shoulder. "Boy, you got to dribble the ball."

Students laughed.

"He's a fuckin' spaz," a muscular kid with his arms folded said. "Look at his skinny white legs. I think he lives under a rock."

Out of nowhere, Martin appeared. He ran up to the kid and smacked him in the face.

"Fight! Fight! Fight!" the others shouted.

Blood poured down the guy's face. Martin sat on top of him, pressing his head against the floor. "You mess with my brother again, and I'll beat the living shit out of you!"

Mr. Hightower separated the two of them. The chubby instructor told his students to continue playing volleyball, then rushed over.

"Can you watch my class?" Mr. Hightower said. "I gotta handle this."

"Sure. Sure."

The three of us were escorted out of the gymnasium. Patrick, the kid Martin punched, was taken to the school nurse by a fidgety slight-framed woman doing hall duty outside the gym. Mr. Hightower brought Martin and me to the headmaster's office.

He explained what happened to the secretary. "Can I leave them with you? I gotta get back to the gym."

"Certainly, Mr. Hightower." She glanced at us and snickered. "Boys, have a seat." She pointed to a row of red plastic chairs, then returned to the papers she was filing in the metal drawers behind her desk.

"Are you crazy?" I whispered to Martin. "You coulda hurt that kid really bad. You looked like a maniac."

Martin laughed. "Guess I'm psycho." He shrugged.

"You didn't need to come over. I could have handled it."

"Fuck that," he said softly. "Anyone tries something with you, they got me to answer to . . . Hey, that rhymes. You should remember that. Put it in one of your stories." He wrapped his arm over my shoulder and pulled me toward him. His T-shirt smelled of sweat and bleach.

The secretary put on silver reading glasses and read a paper. "Glencar, correct? . . . Ah, here it is."

"Yes, I said."

"Here *what* is?" Martin said.

"Your mother's phone number." She picked up the black handset. "Catherine Mulroy?"

"No," Martin said.

"It says it right here."

"That's our grandmother," I said. "I live with her, and my brother lives with my aunt."

"She's listed as the emergency contact. That's who I call."

"My grandmother's at work."

Her forehead creased, and she looked at the paper again. "I see. Says she works at the Mass. General."

"She's a nurse," Martin said. "Maybe she can fix Patrick's nose."

"I don't think you're funny, young man." She told us to shush, then turned her back and spoke quietly into the phone.

She hung up. "She's on her way. And she didn't sound happy. When she gets here, the three of you will have a meeting with Mr. Castellanos."

Mr. Castellanos entered and took us into his office. He asked Martin and me to tell him our side of the story. I heard my grandmother talking to the secretary outside his door. Whenever she was anxious,

Nana spoke loudly. "Glencar is the name. I'm Mrs. Mulroy. I'm here about the fight. You're the one who called me, aren't ya?"

"Yes, ma'am. Have a seat," the woman said.

"I prefer to stand. You'll hurry this up, won't ya? I'm coming from work as you can see. This spot of blood is from a patient who's talking with Saint Peter right now."

The woman opened the door and was about to address Mr. Castellanos, but my grandmother barged past her. "That'll do," she told the woman. "I'll take it from here."

The door slammed.

Mr. Castellanos stood behind his large desk and extended his hand. My grandmother shook it.

"Please sit down, Mrs. Mulroy." He motioned to a maroon cushioned chair. She angled the seat so she could easily look at all of us.

"Can we cut to the bone?"

"Excuse me?" Mr. Castellanos said.

"Hurry it up is what I mean. I had to leave work." She looked at her Timex and pulled on the sides of her white skirt. Her hazel eyes were red rimmed, as though she'd been crying.

"Of course, Mrs. Mulroy. I understand this is an inconvenience for you." Mr. Castellanos put his elbows on his desk and interlocked the fingers of his hands. My grandmother pushed the middle of her large brown glasses over her nose to straighten them. The room filled with the scent of her Shalimar perfume.

"An inconvenience it is," she said, glaring at us.

"Martin assaulted another student."

"Your caked-up secretary told me on the phone that some young man was making fun of Aiden."

Mr. Castellanos twisted his jaw. "Caked up?"

"She wears too much makeup."

"I see." He reclined in his chair and began rubbing the inside of one palm with a thumb. "Boys, tell your grandmother what happened."

Martin recounted the incident. I half listened, embarrassed and humiliated by the whole situation. I looked around the room, trying to distract myself. A line of golden trophies glinted under the buzzing light fixture. There were framed diplomas on the wall behind Mr. Castellanos's desk and a bookshelf under the window to his right with several binders. On top was a vase of half-dead roses. Some of the petals had fallen onto the gray rug. On the wall was a painting of a woman who resembled my mother—long, flame-colored hair and fair skin. She wore an elaborate gown of green, red, and gold. There were vine leaves in the foreground and a large white bird behind her head. She was holding a chalice. The coincidence struck me. Underneath was a gold plaque: "The Damsel of the Holy Grail— *Dante Gabriel Rossetti, 1874.*"

"Isn't that what happened, Aiden?" Martin nudged me.

"Yes." I hadn't been listening.

"Well, it sounds like you did the right thing," my grandmother said, nodding at Martin and smiling.

"The right thing?" Mr. Castellanos clucked his tongue.

"Yes. The right thing," She stared into Mr. Castellanos's eyes. His forehead raised, and he shifted, knocking a picture over.

"Let me help you with that." My grandmother bent over his desk, raising the frame and looking at the photograph. "Isn't he a handsome *divil?*" She placed the picture upright, then sat down.

Mr. Castellanos looked at the pink stain below her right shoulder.

"Blood," she said, looking down. "What a mess it was. We had to crack open the patient's chest to massage his heart."

Mr. Castellanos's cheeks reddened.

"You're one of those people who can't stand the sight of blood. You probably never liked to fight. A pacifist, I suppose?"

He tightened the knot of his tie. "Whether I'm a pacifist or not has nothing to do with the situation at hand."

"And what 'situation at hand' is that?" she said, mocking the gravelly tenor of his voice.

Martin said, "Nana, what I did is wrong." Then to Mr. Castellanos, "I'm sorry, sir. I was sticking up for my brother."

My grandmother picked up the photograph again. "Is this your grandchild?"

"My son." Mr. Castellanos took the picture from her and placed it on the floor behind his desk.

"You look older than I thought . . . Distinguished, though." She smiled. "And does your son have a brother?"

"Yes, two."

"And if one of your sons was being picked on by some ruffian, would you want his brother to kick and boot the brat?"

"I see where you're going with this, Mrs. Mulroy. But the matter at hand is *Martin's* behavior."

She stood. "He did the right thing. And if I were in that smelly gymnasium, I would have hopped on the boy too." She motioned for us to get up. "I suppose you'll be suspending them, will you?"

"School policy is three days of suspension."

"For the both of them?" She took off her glasses and put them in her pocketbook.

"Yes, for any student involved in a fight."

"And what about the other boy. Will you suspend him too?"

"Yes."

"That sounds fair."

"It's the policy."

"Yes, yes. *The policy* . . . I have my own policy."

"What's that?" he said.

"Kick the fucking arse of anyone that goes after your brother." She grabbed a tissue from the box on his desk, spit saliva onto it, then rubbed the blood spot on her uniform. "Where's your wastebasket?"

"Under the desk."

"Should I hand this to you, or would you rather I come 'round and put it in the trash myself?"

"You can put it in the barrel yourself." He picked up his son's photograph, clasped it against his chest, and moved aside. As my grandmother walked over, she noticed the dead flowers in the vase. She shook them into the wastebasket and put the empty vase on his desk.

"Have a good day." She opened the door for us and, before closing it, said, "There are some petals on the rug near the bookcase. You might want to call the janitor."

When we were in the car, Nana said, "I think we need a nice mystery ride."

"Where are we going?" Martin said.

"But that would ruin the mystery." Nana laughed. "You'll like the place."

"I bet it's ice cream," Martin said.

"No, dear, it's not ice cream. Something more special than that."

In a short while we were driving along the Jamaicaway to the Arborway, roads designed by the famous city planner Frederick Law Olmsted. I loved this road with its big, interesting houses. My favorite was a large brick house with lead-paned windows and turrets before the rotary to the Arnold Arboretum.

We parked outside the main gate of our mystery destination—a 281-acre park with over 14,000 different plants and trees, an herbarium collection of 1.3 million specimens, and a huge library. The brick Hunnewell Visitor Center stood like an angel guarding a sacred garden. The air was warm and balmy—Indian summer we called it. A soft breeze with the scent of grass, earth, and decaying vegetation permeated the air. Nana knew where she was headed.

"Follow me, boys." She lit a cigarette and puffed away as we headed along Meadow Road to the intersection of Beech Path, where we walked up a hill past a trash can, then turned right to a tall upright tree with a label that read Pumpkin Ash. I struggled to keep up with

Martin and Nana, who both seemed in better shape than me. I was always perplexed by Nana's energy, considering the way she drank and smoked. Of course, she coughed and spit phlegm often (to which Martin and I would mouth "gross" and laugh), but I admired her verve and strength of purpose; others found her obnoxious. Her friend Rita said she was a difficult woman but loved her just the same. "Difficult people are often the most interesting. In your grandmother's case, her anger is a blessing and a curse." As I grew older, I learned that the source of her rage was a well of sadness.

We turned left and came upon a trunk at least two feet wide.

"Wow, that's so cool. Must be old. Probably as old as you, Nana," Martin said.

"That tree's much older than I. It was probably planted in the early 1800s."

"How do you know all this?" I said.

"Do you think your grandmother is uneducated?"

"I didn't say that, Nana. I'm just curious."

"Sit down."

We sat in a circle under the huge canopy of shade. The air was cooler here, and patches of grass, dirt, and moss surrounded us.

"Aiden, I know about trees because your grandfather and I grew up in the country. And we used to come here when we dated. He would tell me about the different flowers, plants, trees, and wildlife."

She stood and gently pulled a leaf off one of the branches. "See the emerald green color?" She passed the leaf to Martin. He smelled it and pressed it against his cheek, then gave it back to her. She put it in her handbag.

"The color of the leaves reminded us of home. We would come here and talk about our childhoods, life before America. I bet you didn't know that I was a tomboy as a little girl. I loved to climb trees and play outdoors, and I'd spend hours looking for the wee people. Sometimes they pulled on my long red braids."

"The wee people?" Martin said.

"Leprechauns. They hid behind the gorse bushes by the brook I crossed on my way to school. I spotted one of them on a misty morning."

"What did you do?"

"I ran after him, Aiden."

"Why?"

"I wanted to know where the pot of gold was."

Martin laughed. "Nana. There's no such thing as leprechauns."

"Don't be so sure. Nothing in life is certain. Except for one thing."

"What's that?" I said.

"Love . . . And God is love." Leaves rustled. She looked up. "Feel the breeze. That could be the Holy Spirit."

Martin grinned at me.

"Your grandfather always said that the best place to find God was in nature. I believe he was right."

We were silent for a bit. A woodpecker knocked on bark in the distance, and water rushed in a stream at the bottom of the slope. A Baltimore oriole whistled from the wide treetop above, like a singing flame of fire.

"Did you know this tree is holy?" Nana said. "Prayers spoken under it go directly to heaven. And beech trees know all about the past. Many people believe that the first literature was written on beech tree bark."

Martin said, "Aiden, start collecting some pages. I don't know if the bark will fit in your typewriter, though." He laughed.

"Isn't it graceful? Such strength . . . Get off your arses and stand with me while I tell you a few things."

I brushed my pants where some moss had stuck. Martin put his arm around Nana. I joined him. The three of us looked at the verdant spread of leaves above us. Two squirrels hissed, then one chased the other.

"All God's creatures have disagreements. Which brings me to what I want to discuss with you." She wiped her skirt.

"I'm a bit embarrassed about my behavior today. My Irish was up. I was disrespectful to your headmaster, and I shouldn't have been. The man is just doing his job." She dropped her cigarette to the ground and stepped on it.

She looked at Martin. "What you did was right. Always look out for your loved ones. Like a tree." She looked around. "A person can only be as strong as the family that surrounds it." She turned. "How do you think these trees survive?"

Martin shrugged. He was getting bored and kicked a rock.

"When one tree gets sick or hurt, it depends on the strength of those near it. Underneath the surface of this dirt is a large network of intersecting roots. These roots keep each tree alive by intertwining. They create a sturdy foundation so the family of trees remains strong." She waved her arm. "This chain of trees is only as strong as its weakest link. Trees do not hesitate to help each other. They stick together and share their strength. This is what love is all about."

Martin and I looked at the foliage. "Inhale the beauty," my grandmother said. We took deep breaths, then followed Nana back to the car.

On the trail back, Nana announced, "Your mother is coming for a visit this weekend."

Martin and I sped up.

Chapter Six

We drove to Aunt Clara's to drop off Martin. When we were parked in front, Nana turned and said, "You can come in if you want to, or you can sit in the car."

"I'll wait here."

"Don't blame ya. Herself will probably have a fit that she wasn't notified." She looked at Martin next to her. "Didn't you write her name on the emergency card?"

Martin said, "Nah. She makes a big deal outta nothing. I wanted you as the contact."

Nana patted his head. "Good boy . . . Let's go in."

Martin punched me playfully. "See ya."

They headed up the walkway, deep in conversation. I grabbed a bottled water from a cooler on the floor of the back seat and watched them. Nana did most of the talking. Martin nodded. She must have been telling him what to say and how to handle the situation. My grandmother was a take-charge person. What would we do without her? The realization that someday she'd die saddened me, and my eyes filled. I heard a loud bang on the trunk. The car bounced up and down. I saw nothing and opened the door. Maybe a branch fell from the oak tree? When I reached the bumper, the woman in the floral dress sprang up. "Pussy!" She pointed to the water in my hand. "One day you'll choke on that. You may even die. Would serve you well. Teach your kin not to steal another's water." I felt my heart jump a beat. I stepped back and almost tripped.

She twisted a long strand of gray hair with a finger and looked at the sky. "Now I live in a land where there is no water. God help me," she cried. The whites of her eyes were completely red, and that foul smell filled the air. She pressed a skinny finger into my chest. Her hands were a grimy black, the long nails sharp and ridged with the sickly orange hue of a chain smoker. Lumpy knuckles protruded from her gray veiny skin. She opened her thin-lipped mouth and laughed hoarsely. "You helpless little poof. Your brother won't always be 'round to protect ya." She pouted and spoke in a baby voice. Her wide gray eyes seemed to glow.

"Why are you bothering me?"

A blob of shit dropped on her shoulder. A cardinal chirped on the branch above, leaping to and fro. She wiped the excrement with her finger and licked it. "Tastes as good as poke." She laughed. "Vanilla with a little chocolate. My favorite."

"Who the fuck are you?"

"Moira le Fay."

"Why don't you leave me alone? I don't know you."

"But I've known ya family for generations. Your kin disturbed my well and stole my berries. You make me sick." She growled, and the indentation above her bluish clavicle trembled. She sighed. "I hate you all."

"Keep the fuck away from me."

She spit. "Such a nasty lad."

I opened the car door. She hugged me and scraped my forearms with her nails. Lines oozed blood.

"Now we're twins."

I grimaced and slammed the door on her hand. A finger dropped on the rug. I ground my sneaker on it until it was a pile of dust. She sucked the stump and pounded my window with her other hand. I couldn't see her. I locked the doors and looked up and down the street. She was gone.

I closed my eyes and fell asleep. My mother and I were looking at a mist-covered mountain across a bay.

My grandmother tapped on the window. "Unlock the door."

I pulled the knob. A soft breeze blew in.

"Why did you lock the door?"

"I don't know."

She looked at me suspiciously.

"What a scene." She stared forward. "That woman drives me mad. What's most important is that Martin is all right. She was spouting that *shite* about Jesus and the other cheek." She turned to look at me. "I know Jesus said we should turn the other cheek. He was a good man, but I don't agree with everything he said."

Her eyes lowered. "What happened to you?" She grabbed my arms. "Why do you scratch yourself so? Are you nervous?"

"No."

"*Scundered* about what happened today?" I must have looked confused. "Embarrassed."

"No."

"Then why are you so out of sorts?" She studied my arms. "You're bleeding."

"I get itchy sometimes."

She breathed deeply and exhaled while shaking her head. "I don't believe you. Mothers and grandmothers always know when their children lie." She started the car. "It's all right, sweetheart. You'll tell me when you're ready. I'll put cortisone cream on those arms when we get home." In the rearview mirror, I saw her eyebrows draw together, worried and wondering.

My grandmother rubbed the cortisone into my skin. Later, we ate burgers and her homemade french fries cooked in bacon grease. Even now, I can see her shaking the fries in the paper bag. She always said, "You're going to love these," and I did.

After dinner, we watched the 1960 film *The Time Machine*, based on the novel by H. G. Wells. She fell asleep on the couch, her glasses on her chest, a cigarette burning in the ashtray, and a tumbler of whiskey on the coffee table. I shook her gently and told her I was going to bed.

"I can't find you," she said. "Where are you, Ma?"

"Nana, it's Aiden."

She sat up and rubbed her eyes. "Hand me my drink. I was dreaming."

"About what?"

"My ma."

She gulped whiskey and wiped her mouth. "You and Laura remind me of her." She looked at the drawing of the old man on the wall. "Why was your mother so obsessed with him?" I refused to look at that sketch. People said it was one of Mom's best drawings, but I didn't want to remember the chaos the "ghost" created. Nana liked the drawing, even with the drama that surrounded it. She felt she knew the man and said he seemed kind.

"'He's so sad. I've got to help him,' Laura kept saying." She put her hand on my knee. "A figment of her imagination? Someone we knew? How curious the mind is. Mental illness is a terrible thing."

"Maybe Mom isn't crazy," I blurted.

"What are ya saying?" She tilted her head.

"Maybe she can see things that most of us can't. Like second sight. What *your* mother had."

Her leg banged against the coffee table, and her drink spilled.

"Who told you about my mother?" She took a newspaper from the floor and sopped up the whiskey.

"You did."

"Did I?" Her eyes looked up. She crumpled the newspaper, leaving it on the table, then finished the last of her drink.

"A long time ago." I tamped out her cigarette. She never told me about her mother, but I couldn't tell her Grandpa did.

"That's funny. I don't remember."

"You're old."

She laughed. "You're a brat. Off to bed. You've got school in the morning."

"I'm suspended. Remember?"

"Jaysus. Maybe I *am* getting senile. Grab my arm and help me to the stairs."

When we reached the first step and her hand was on the bannister, I kissed her cheek. "Good night."

"You'll be all right on your own tomorrow, won't ya?"

"You asked me that earlier."

"Right." She began climbing the stairs.

I stood beside her.

"I'm fine. Go to bed." She waved me onward.

I heard her muttering, "He'll be OK. I wish you were still here, Sean. Ma, I'm so sorry."

At 11:37, my grandfather visited. I was glad because I had questions to ask. Again, my face flushed, and bubbles of light appeared.

"I know you have questions."

"Who is that blonde lady at school?"

"We call her a shimmerer. A good soul who has passed. Before she completes her journey, she has something she wants to accomplish."

"What does she want?"

"She's watching over her daughter."

"Hope Gallagher?"

"Yes, son."

"Why does she need to watch over her?"

"You'll find out."

"You're not going to tell me?"

He laughed. "Curiosity killed the cat."

"I don't have a cat."

"There's a cat somewhere. You don't want him to die, do you?"

"Maybe he's dead *and* alive." I laughed.

"Yes, he is. It would depend on your vantage point."

"Mom's coming home this weekend."

"Good. You've got to convince Martin to get her out of that hospital." He crossed himself. "I hope she makes a pretense of 'sanity' for Catherine."

"But she *is* sane."

"You and I know that, but most people don't understand. They're afraid when things don't fit their idea of reality. The problem with the world is most people are too rigid. They think they know what's real, but their vision is limited." He leaned forward. "If Laura does something that others think peculiar, you must protect her. Make her actions seem rational."

"How?"

"You're smart, Aiden. You'll think of a way. Use that imagination of yours."

"Maybe you're part of my imagination. Maybe *I'm* crazy."

"'I am certain of nothing but the holiness of the heart's affections and the truth of imagination,' a poet once said. Remember that."

"Grandpa, how can Martin and I help Mom escape by ourselves? We're kids. We don't drive."

"Get Margie to help. And Rita—she's clever. Tell her I asked for her assistance."

"But she won't believe me."

"Tell her I said, 'Thanks for finding Catherine's pearls between the car seats.' Only she and I know about that." He laughed. "Say I kidded her about praying to Saint Anthony before she went to the car."

He told me another story about the particulars of his death and said I would know the right time and place to reveal the details.

The room became dark, and my grandfather disappeared.

"I've made you an omelet. Come down," Nana called.

I was reading the Bible in bed, trying to figure out why God had been so exacting in his directions to Noah about building the ark. The ship had to be made out of cypress wood, 450 feet long, 75 feet wide, and 45 feet high. And how could Noah fit all those creatures on one boat?

I put on jeans and a shirt, then washed my face and flattened my hair with water.

She was on the phone, its long extension cord stretched to where she stood at the stove. She adjusted the burner and moved the pan. When she heard me pull the chair out, she turned and put her finger against her lips. She was wearing her favorite nightgown—a pattern of purple heather and yellow flowers.

"Yes, yes, I realize why you're upset." She motioned for me to pour some orange juice. The air smelled of bacon grease and cigarette smoke. Sparrows rose in the air outside the window.

"He could have. I promise you I'll have a talk with him. . . Thank you for that . . . He's doing OK. The doctor says he's in full remission . . . Amen to that. God *does* work in mysterious ways . . . I'll call you back. He's just come down for his breakfast."

She brought me a plate with a cheddar cheese omelet, home fries, and bacon.

"Will you have coffee?"

"Yes, please."

She took a mug from the cabinet and poured. "Grab the cream, will ya?"

When we were both seated, I asked, "Aren't you gonna eat?"

"I ate already."

I knew she hadn't. I worried about her health—all her smoking, that persistent cough, and her lousy diet.

"Margie's having a conniption over that jewelry. I knew it was only a matter of time, but I thought she wouldn't discover it missing for a while. Her place is such a pigsty. I don't think she moves her fat arse from that chair in her parlor."

"Maybe she's depressed?"

"Could be. She's always been a sad person. Not too bright either." She looked out the window. "I love those birds." The sparrows were splashing themselves in the gutter along the shed roof. It had poured during the night.

"What are you gonna tell her about the jewelry?" I said.

"That you took it." She sipped her coffee and looked down.

"We've got to return it, Nana. And the chalice too. I don't think it's right that we stole them."

"And who are you to tell me what's wrong or right? Mind your manners and eat up. Your food will get cold."

She was always watching me as though she had a question. Martin said she could see right into us.

"What were ya doing when I called ya?"

"Reading about the Flood."

"You're a funny one." She laughed.

"I can't make any sense of it."

"Make sense of what, Aiden?"

"God sounds like an architect when he tells Noah to build the ark."

"God *is* an architect. Of you, me, the world, even those birds."

We watched the sparrows in silence. The trees behind them swayed in the wind.

"Give me your plate if you're finished. I'll put the leftovers outside for the birds."

I looked at the remaining potatoes. "Nana, I don't think birds like potatoes."

"Stop being so obnoxious. You don't know more than me." She opened the door off the kitchen and put the plate on a step.

When she returned, she said, "I will tell Margie we had a talk, and you 'fessed up."

"But it was your idea!"

She slapped the table. My coffee spilled.

"Apologize," she yelled, her cheeks red.

"Sorry." I wiped the coffee up with my napkin.

"I didn't hear you."

"Sorry," I said loudly.

"That's better . . . This is what we'll do." She washed the pan in the sink, her back to me. "Since you're expelled, you'll return the jewelry while I'm at work."

I refrained from correcting her and saying "suspended."

"It was a load of crap anyway."

"What was?"

"The jewelry . . . All fake. Even the sapphire ring that Arthur gave her."

"Her cat gave her a ring?"

She laughed deeply and coughed. "No, darling. Her high school boyfriend."

"Margie had a boyfriend."

"Yes. I think he pitied her. She wasn't always so fat and sad. Poor thing. She was quite the looker when your grandfather and I first met her years ago . . . Come over here and dry this pan and the mugs while I talk to you."

I grabbed the towel from the refrigerator handle and joined her.

"I'm sorry for eating your head off."

"What?"

"Losing my patience. That wasn't right." She passed me a mug. "I've got a terrible temper. Always have. And I'm stubborn."

"It's OK."

"No, it's not . . . My father had a temper too. But not my mother. She was lovely, like Laura . . . And you." She bent over and held my cheeks. "I adore you, sweetheart." Her hands were wet and warm. She looked sad. "I wish I was nicer to my mother. But I was a young girl."

"All children are pains," I said.

She laughed. "Do you love me?"

"Yes, Nana. Of course I love you."

"Are you OK with our little white lie? You'll return the jewelry? Except for the gold necklace. I can't take that from your mother. She needs it, and what would I say to Laura? Think of some excuse when you go to Margie's house today."

"I will."

"I know ya will." She put her hands on my shoulders. "And you *are* smarter than me, Aiden. That's the truth." She playfully hit my butt. "Go change your shirt. You've got cheese and egg on it. I need to finish cleaning up and get ready for work. But first I'll call Margie and tell her that you're coming. That you were worried about money for your mother's hospital costs."

I pushed in my chair. She moved closer to the window. The birds had flown away.

"That will be our story," I said.

I heard the front door close, went to the bedroom window, and watched my grandmother drive off. I changed into black corduroy pants and a gray-and-white checkered shirt.

Margie lived on Wren Street, north of Nana's and past Rita's place, which I passed along the way.

Her white house needed fixing up. The porch screens were ripped, one of the gutters had fallen, and tufts of weeds grew between the cement blocks in her front walk. I checked my Timex, which read 11:00 a.m., and wondered if she was drinking yet. Rita was a former English professor. My grandmother told me Rita and my grandfather loved to talk about writers and books. They would often recite their favorite poems and literary passages.

After her husband died, she retired. "No need to work," she once said. "My husband left me well off, but I'd give all the money I have to see him again. I'd give the same amount to be with your grandfather, discussing literature, seeing his beautiful face across the table."

The air was crisp, and leaves blew like somebody's trash across the sidewalk and into the street. Margie would be sitting in her overstuffed chair with Arthur on her lap. She had never married, and her father, perhaps because he felt sorry for her, bought her a big house, too big for one person and a pet.

I had been practicing what I would say on the walk over. When she opened the door, Arthur ran out as usual, probably trying to escape the depressing and dingy aura of the place. I caught him. All the blinds were down, except for those in the kitchen down the hall. In the living room, the TV blared the soap opera *The Young and the Restless*. I heard the voices of two women arguing over a man.

"Have a seat with me, Aiden." She patted the couch next to her.

"These two are like cats in heat. Gonna scratch each other's eyes out. All for a man." She placed Arthur on her fat belly and smoothed his hair. He blinked at me.

"Nana says you had a boyfriend named Arthur."

"Why would she tell you that?"

I shrugged. "Guess she was trying to make conversation."

She patted the cat more vigorously. "Sometimes Catherine don't know when to keep her mouth shut."

I placed the bag of jewelry between us. Her eyes were glued to the TV, where a blonde woman had exited and slammed a door.

"These stories make me laugh. All so dumb." She took the jewelry out of the bag. "These pieces ain't worth shit. Sentimental value . . . Aren't you gonna apologize?"

I laughed.

"What's so funny?" She looked at me sideways.

"You're so direct. Makes me laugh."

"Is that bad?"

I loved her childlike quality. "It's good that you make me laugh, Margie. And yes, I'm sorry. I was worried that Nana couldn't keep up with my mother's hospital bills."

She peered into the bag. "Where's the gold cross?"

"We gave it to Mom."

Margie sighed. "I suppose it will do her more good than me . . . I'm not sure I even believe in God." As she stood up, she said, "Ouch. This goddamn back." She turned off the television. "Follow me . . . Let's eat somethin'. And don't tell Catherine what I said about God. She's a holy roller."

She had one of the widest asses I'd seen. Arthur's hairs formed a snowflake on her navy-blue pants. I wanted to pick some off but knew that would be rude.

In the kitchen, which was bright compared to the dungeon-like atmosphere of the rest of her house, she put a kettle of tea on the stove.

"You want some cookies? They're my favorite . . . I like to dip them in the tea till they get all mushy and fall apart . . . Like life." She chuckled.

"Sure." I pulled out a chair. A plate with toast crust was on the table, as well as a glass half full of orange juice.

"If your grandmother was here, she would tell me I was wasting food and some shit about children starving in Africa. She ever play that guilt trip on you?"

I laughed. "Many times."

The kettle whistled, and she poured us Irish breakfast tea. I took milk out of the refrigerator and grabbed the red sugar bowl from the counter.

"I like a man that takes charge," she said, huffing as she sat down and poured the milk. She bit into a cookie. "I gotta lose weight."

I sipped.

"You're supposed to say, 'No, you don't, Margie'" She slapped my hand playfully.

I said the tea was good.

"You put enough sugar in it."

I stared at her. "Maybe you should go for a walk every evening." I looked out the window. "Fall is perfect weather."

She waved her hand and sipped more tea. "Why bother? No man is gonna look at me. I enjoy being fat. It's my revenge."

"Revenge for what?"

"Arthur dropping me like a fat potato."

"You mean *hot* potato."

"No, I mean *fat*. I was one of the prettiest girls in high school, then I started eating a lot. My mother said I was trying to compensate for a void inside me." She bit another cookie. Black crumbs fell onto her lap. Arthur licked them up. "My mother was a psychologist. I still don't know what that phrase 'God rest her soul' means, but I guess you're supposed to say it. She fell into a manhole in front of Filenes on Washington Street. Broke her neck. Guess she learned about voids real good." She laughed. "They were doing construction on a broken pipe."

"You must have felt awful."

"Not really. I hated her. She was mean. Always picking on me. Not that I wanted her dead, but I can't say I was upset when she fell underground. That's where we all end up anyway, right?" She forced a smile. "Holes in the ground."

"I guess so."

"Help me clear these dishes. Why aren't you in school, by the way?"

"One of the kids was calling me names during gym class. Martin heard him and punched the guy in the face."

Her eyes watered. "Good. It ain't right when people are mean." She patted my head.

"Margie, will you help Martin and me plan an escape for my mother?"

She bent down and looked me in the eyes. "Your mother's sick, honey."

"No, she isn't"

"Didn't she go looney? Talking nonsense about ghosts?"

"I think she sees things that other people don't."

"Ain't possible. I never seen a ghost."

"Maybe someday you will." I turned away and sat at the table.

"Hope I don't see my mother ... You read too many scary books, Aiden. I never had that problem. Couldn't make it through one book in all my years at school. TV is more fun . . . Come on, let's go back in and see what happens between those two bitches."

"Will you help me save my mother?"

"You love your mom a lot, don't you?"

"Yes."

"Does your grandmother know what you boys have in mind?"

"No. And she can't. She thinks Mom is sick."

"Don't you want Laura to get better?"

"She *is* better."

"You sound so sure." We were sitting on the couch again. The TV camera zoomed in on a brunette gazing longingly out a window. It was raining, and tears slid down her cheeks.

Margie pointed. "I like her better than the other one."

"Are you gonna help us?"

She squeezed Arthur, and he meowed. "Sure."

"Our secret, right?"

"Yes, Aiden. Our secret . . . It will force me to get outta this dump. Someday I'm gonna die in this chair . . . Promise me something?"

"Yes."

"If anything happens to me, you'll take care of Arthur."

I reached over to pet him. He hissed. "I will, Margie."

Chapter Seven

My mother came home Saturday morning. Martin and I waited on the front lawn, our eyes darting up and down the street as we looked for my grandmother's Plymouth. When they arrived, Martin rushed to hug Mom as she opened the car door. I walked toward her slowly.

"Aiden, aren't you excited to see me?" Her expression was puzzled. Behind the car stood the old lady ghost, Moira, who laughed, exposing yellow, rotten teeth. My mother turned to look.

"What are you staring at, honey?"

"Nothing." I moved quickly. She hugged me and smiled. "I can't believe I'm with you boys." The cotton of her green pants and paisley red blouse smelled of Ivory soap and Avon perfume. Her hands were warm.

The old woman vanished.

"Let's get inside. It's time to celebrate." Nana walked around the front of the car. Four seagulls circled in the sky, as if watching over us. A cool breeze smelled of ozone. Nana looked up. The sky darkened in the west. "A storm's coming. We're all *delira* and *excira*, but if we stay outside, we'll be soaking wet." A few drops fell.

My mother wrapped her arm around my grandmother's back. "I've always loved your Irish expressions. They make me feel so at home."

"You *are* home, darling." They walked toward the front door. Mom leaned her head against Nana's shoulder.

While they made dinner, Martin and I sat on the living room rug and played the board game *Risk.* Our armies fought to take possession of countries. I blocked his armies in Iceland by conquering Scandinavia and Europe.

"At least I have Great Britain." He placed his index finger on the board. "And that includes Ireland. Ha!"

Martin was obsessed with Irish history and culture. West Roxbury was home to the "lace-curtain Irish," those Irish who were allegedly better off than their fellow immigrants in South Boston. Home, family, and tradition defined him. I was less impassioned about my heritage and couldn't wait to explore the world. I loved my family, but I felt like an outsider. Irish Catholics were repressed and stoical. I knew I could never survive in my hometown.

We held hands as my grandmother said grace. She closed her eyes and prayed. "Thank you, Jesus, for all the wonderful people in our lives, especially my beautiful daughter."

We began the silent ritual of dinner, eating juicy steak and baked potatoes. In our household, talk during meals was not encouraged, especially when my father was around.

Mom placed a potato on her dish. "I want to tell you about my new friend at the place." The words *hospital* and *psychiatric facility,* we all understood, were taboo.

"Her name is Nell." Her green eyes lit up. She pushed hair off her shoulder. The red spot, a sign of excitement, appeared in the center of her forehead. "You'd like her, Aiden. She loves to tell stories. And she used to be a nightclub singer."

My grandmother served us more green beans. "How did she end up in that place?"

"Poor woman. One night she had a panic attack onstage and hasn't been able to perform since. She suffers with anxieties and other phobias."

"That's sad," I said. "I feel sorry for her."

"You're a sensitive young man." My mother smiled and touched my hand.

"A little too sensitive." My grandmother sat down.

"You can never be too sensitive, Ma."

My grandmother carved into her steak.

Mom examined my face. "Nana told me a boy at school was making fun of you."

"I suck at sports. We were playing basketball, and I screwed up."

"What the world needs now is love, sweet love," she sang. "Ignore hateful people." Her eyes glistened.

"Amen," my grandmother said.

"I second that." Martin winked at me.

"Be proud of who you are. You don't need to be like everyone else. If we were all the same, life would be dull." My mother leaned over and kissed my cheek.

Nana said, "It's true, Aiden. I can cook and clean, but I'm not bright like your grandfather was. He loved me anyway."

"You're smart, Nana," I said.

She spread her hands. "You all know things that I don't."

My mother looked at me. I think she was afraid I might say something about our visions.

"Reading is the best way to learn," Mom said.

My grandmother cleared our plates. "Your grandfather loved his books."

My mother said, "I'm happy you kept all his things."

"I will never change that room. His books bring me comfort . . . Time for another drink. You want one, Laura?"

"No thanks, Ma."

My grandmother poured another whiskey. Later, Mom helped her dry dishes. Martin and I went to my room.

"I spoke with Margie the other day." We were sitting on my bed. Martin was trying to place a rifle in the hands of a G.I. Joe.

"I want to join the army someday."

"Dad wouldn't like that. He wants us to go to college," I said.

He propped himself against the wall with a pillow. "I'm not college material."

"That's not true. You don't try hard enough."

"'Cause it doesn't interest me. I'd rather fight mean people. Mom's right. Too many assholes in the world."

"Margie says she'll help us get Mom out of that place."

He threw the G.I. Joe onto the floor. "Aiden, I keep telling you, Mom's not ready."

"She is."

"How can you be so sure?"

"That place will kill her. Turn her into a zombie or something."

"Don't be so dramatic. The doctors are helping her."

"No, they aren't. There's nothing wrong with her." I felt my ears get hot.

"You're certain?" He leaned forward.

"Yes. Life would be boring if everyone was the same. Just like Mom said." My voice cracked.

"What did Margie say?"

"That she'd help. We have to think this through."

"We should use her cat. What's its name? Archie?" He rubbed his hands together.

"Arthur."

"He can be our feint."

"The cat can't faint." I laughed.

"A feint is a military maneuver where you draw your enemy's attention to something that doesn't matter."

"A distraction?"

"Exactly. That cat is wild. Always hissing and scratching. Margie could bring him to the hospital. Get those nurses to say how cute he is, even though we know they'll think he's fat as shit." He laughed. "But they gotta be nice, especially to an old lady. When they start petting him, he'll bite or scratch them. That's when we make our move."

"What's that?"

"While they deal with the scratched nurse, we take Mom down the stairs at the end of the hall." He rubbed his chin with his thumb. "We need to have someone in a getaway car."

"I can talk to Nana's friend, Rita."

"Are we gonna tell Nana?" Martin said.

"No. She'd never allow it."

"But she'll be mad if we do it. And what do we say when we bring her home?"

"Let me worry about that," I said. "I'll convince her it was the right thing to do."

"She listens to you, Aiden."

"Sometimes."

"Most of the time. You know things. What other stuff do you know, Mr. Vision Man?"

"I know you better head to Aunt Clara's . . ."

"Clarise," he said, affecting a French accent.

"If you don't go soon, she'll call and bitch at Nana."

"I sorta feel sorry for Aunt Clara. She wanted a different life. Always watching old movies." He jumped off the bed and stretched.

"You feel sorry for everyone."

He laughed. "Not everyone. I'll go so 'Herself' doesn't have a hissy fit." He imitated my grandmother.

"Don't tell anyone about our idea." I walked with him down the hall.

"What idea?" He turned and winked.

Later, I went to the living room. My grandmother, mother, and I watched *The Sonny and Cher Show*. They were performing, "Rescue

Me." The line "'Cause I'm lonely and I'm blue" confirmed for me that we were doing the right thing.

I arrived at Rita's house about noon. Her blue eyes widened when she opened the door. She patted the sides of her red hair and smoothed her pleated cotton nightdress, a pattern of honeybees. She was always donning unusual clothing or changing the color of her hair, which was ash blonde a few months ago.

"Aiden, I'm a mess. I fell asleep on the couch. Come in."

She held a book entitled *Audrey Rose*. She saw me looking at the cover. A girl in a red dress stood in front of a grave. The ground was on fire.

"Junk. I hope you're reading better things in school . . . What grade are you in this year? Old people lose track of time. The years merge together and sometimes they seem to disappear." She laughed.

"Ninth."

"Before I know it, you'll be in college." She rubbed my head. "Let's sit in the backyard. It's such a lovely day."

We walked through the hallway and kitchen to a brick patio covered by a pergola. She led me to a black wrought-iron table. Sunlight flickered through the red cedar lattice above us, dappling her face. The air smelled grassy and pungent. Cat urine? I smelled roses too.

"Will ya have a cup of tea?" She pulled out a rusted chair.

"Sure."

"Sit here. I'll be back in a jiff."

A blue jay lapped the greenish water of a fluted cement birdbath, then shook its wings, cawed, and flew away. Along one side of the patio, potted plants moved in the breeze; a few swayed in macramé holders—ferns dropping tears of moisture, the yellow-and-green spider plant, the wandering Jew with its purple-and-green heart-shaped leaves, and some I could not name. Children laughed on the other side of the tall hedge. Hanging on the fence was a metal plaque with a quote my grandfather recited during one of his visits: "Goodness is the only investment that never fails."

"Grab this for me, will you?" Rita elbowed the screen door. She held a small tray with a teapot, two cups, milk, and sugar.

As I hurried toward her, a brown mouse or small rat darted in front of me.

"Thank you, Aiden."

When we were seated, she said, "Isn't this peaceful?" She looked around. "Sometimes I sit here from morning until evening, watching the birds lift their wings or listening till the crickets sing." She laughed. "I'm a poet." She laughed again and poured tea into a cup with milk and sugar. "Here you go." Then she poured her own. A small pot of azaleas cast a purple glow under her chin.

"I want to apologize," I said.

"For what?" She sipped and looked at me over her tea.

"Nana and I lied to you."

"And when did you do that?"

"I don't have leukemia."

"I know that, Aiden," she said matter-of-factly.

"If you knew my grandmother was lying, why did you write the check?"

"Your grandmother is a lifelong friend. She needed money. I recognized her anxiety and wanted to help."

"Aren't you mad?"

"Of course not. Catherine lies." She looked away. "But we all do. To others and to ourselves." A shadow passed over her face. "'Life is a tale of human frailty and sorrow.' Do you know who said that?"

"Shakespeare?"

She smiled. "Good guess. But it was Nathaniel Hawthorne in *The Scarlet Letter*. You'll read the book in high school." She scrutinized my face. "You're not here to talk about school. To what do I owe the honor of your visit, dear Aiden?" She put her elbows on the table and rested her chin in her hands.

"What was that book about? Not *The Scarlet Letter*. The one you were holding when I came to the front door."

"It's about a man who loses his wife and daughter in a terrible car crash. He's heartbroken, so he goes to a psychic to get solace."

"What does the psychic tell him?"

"She tells him that his daughter has been reincarnated as Ivy Templeton, a girl living in New York City. He sets out to find her, but you'll have to read the book to find out what happens."

"Tell me."

"It would ruin the surprise. If we knew endings, life would be mundane, don't you think?"

My hand shook a little as I drank the tea. "You sound like Grandpa."

"How do you know what Sean sounded like? He died before you were born."

"Rita, do you believe there's life after death?"

"I tend to think not."

"Do you believe in ghosts?"

"I've never seen one, and I don't know anyone besides your mother who has claimed to." She sipped.

I was quiet.

Furrows appeared in her forehead. "Have you seen a ghost, Aiden?" She laughed and put her cup down.

"Maybe."

"Either you have or you haven't. Which is it?" She reached across the table and grabbed my hand. "Tell me about your ghost. I love stories."

"My grandfather."

"Sean?" She sighed. "I miss your grandfather."

"Ghosts are true."

"Aiden, you have an active imagination."

I must have looked annoyed. She smiled.

"I believe you *think* you saw Sean's ghost . . . Don't be angry with me." She poured more tea into my cup. "Shall I get you some cookies?" She was about to get up.

"He came to me at night. He said my mother doesn't belong at McCall's, and we should help her escape. He told me to ask you for help because you always know what to do. You fix things."

"Aiden, your mother's ill. You were dreaming about your grandfather."

"He said my mother isn't crazy." I looked down. "And neither am I. He told me we both have second sight."

Her face paled. She moved her chair to my side of the table and put her arm around my shoulder. "Ya know what I think?" Her eyes shone. I smelled beer. "I think you have a creative mind, and you should write stories. The Irish are known for their literature." She threaded my hair with her fingers. "You've got his hair. And you're so much like him with your curious ways." She patted my knee. "Help me clean up." She rose and placed our cups on the tray with the teapot. "Hold the door open."

"Grandpa wanted me to thank you for helping him find my grandmother's pearls. He said he laughed at you for praying to Saint Anthony before you went to the car. You found the necklace between the seats."

She dropped the tray. Bits of blue and white china smashed on the bricks. A linnet swooped down and sat on the birdbath.

Her shoulders trembled. She pointed to the birdbath. "That was your grandfather's favorite bird." She wiped tears from her cheeks.

I felt awkward and stooped to pick up the mess.

"You'll cut yourself. Sit at the table with me."

The linnet flew to a crossbeam above us and looked down as if it were listening to our conversation. He cleaned his reddish breast with his beak.

"How did you know about the necklace? Did you read something in one of your grandfather's journals?"

"I didn't know my grandfather wrote in journals."

Her chin jutted forward, and she fingered her collar. "Aiden, I'm trying to discern how you learned these things. Sean and I were the only people who knew about the pearls." She smiled, glancing at the linnet, preoccupied with memory. "Did he tell you why he was giving your grandmother the necklace?"

"No."

"It was their first anniversary. Your grandmother was due home any minute. I had helped him prepare a nice dinner—filet mignon, green beans almandine, baked potatoes, and a fancy salad with croutons and anchovies. He went to his closet to get the pearls and came back in a panic. I prayed aloud to Saint Anthony. Sean laughed at me, but when I returned from the car, he was joyous."

"Do you believe me now?"

She covered her lips with two fingers and stared. "Maybe . . . I suppose anything is possible."

The bird swooped in front of us and flew away.

Rita touched her chest. "He startled me."

"Will you help then?" I said.

"Help what?"

"Rescue my mother."

Rita twisted her lips and pondered. "We've got to ask Margie to assist. We need more than the two of us."

"I already did. She agreed. Martin did too."

Rita put her hand on mine. "OK. We'll meet here to come up with a strategy." She looked at the clock. "You better leave. Your grandmother will wonder where you are. You mustn't tell her anything. She's stubborn."

"My mother is visiting from the hospital."

"Why are you here, Aiden? You should be spending time with your ma."

"Nana took her to church."

Rita laughed. "I'm sure Laura was thrilled. And on a Saturday too!"

"My mother doesn't agree with the church. She said they screwed it all up once Saint Paul and Saint Augustine got involved."

"I was kidding. I know Laura was never one for organized religion, though she's always loved to read and study the Bible. She's a good daughter. Trying to make your grandmother happy. You and your brother come here after school on Monday. Where is Martin now?"

"Probably swimming at the YMCA. Then back to Aunt Clara's."

When we were at the front door, Rita said, "I'll call Margie. You speak with Martin. Will fried bologna sandwiches do? I know how you boys like those. Your grandfather's favorite." She smiled.

"Any food is good."

She opened the storm door. "Hurry along."

I ran down the steps and turned once to look at her. She waved, wiping more tears from her cheeks. I thought how great is the power of love and memory.

Chapter Eight

After I passed the overgrown front lawn of the McDermotts' place, my grandmother's house came into view. Nana was standing at the back of a white-and-orange ambulance emblazoned with blue "Boston EMS: Emergency Medical Services" and "911." Some neighbors had gathered. I ran.

Martin's and my grandmother's backs faced me. He rubbed his hand on the space between her shoulders. My mother waved to me from a stretcher that was about to be lifted into the back of the vehicle. The paramedics, a tall black-haired woman with a tight ponytail and a stocky, cherubic-faced man with a red beard, looked up when I shouted, "What happened?"

Both Martin and Nana turned.

"It's nothing," my mother said. "I had a little fall from the tree." She was cupping her left elbow. Her face looked pained.

"A tree?"

The paramedics moved aside so I could get to her stretcher. They folded their arms, and the woman said something into a walkie-talkie. I heard the words "vital signs" and "probable fracture" but couldn't make out the rest.

"It's *not* nothing," Nana snapped. Her nostrils flared, and the area around her mouth trembled.

"She'll be OK." Martin looked up at her.

"By the grace of God." Nana looked toward the sun. "You might have broken your neck, become paralyzed."

"Mom, you always think the worst." She looked down at her arm. Pine needles lay in her hair, and her pink blouse was stained with dirt and grass.

"You're too carefree, Laura!"

Martin moved back and put his hand over my shoulder. "She'll be all right."

The female paramedic said, "We gotta get moving, folks," and lifted the stretcher. "Does one of you want to accompany her in the back of the ambulance? We're headed to the Mass. General. That's what you wanted, Ms. . . . I'm sorry, I forget your name."

"Mulroy. Catherine Mulroy . . . I'm a nurse there."

"I'll go in the ambulance," Martin said.

My mother clapped her hands and smiled, then winced. "The ride will be fun, sweetheart. Speeding away, listening to sirens."

"We'll follow." My grandmother pulled me to her car.

"We'll be moving fast," the man said. "Don't try to keep up with us."

"I'm well aware of that, young man. I know how to get to my place of work."

Martin jumped in. My mother and he waved before the paramedics shut the back doors. As the EMTs opened their doors, my grandmother said, "We'll see you in the ER. Be careful of the traffic. We don't need another accident."

The woman smiled wanly. The man said, "Yup."

On the ride over, I asked my grandmother what happened.

"Your mother thought she saw a girl in a green pinafore stuck in that pine tree by the corner of the house."

"What's a pinafore?"

"An old-fashioned dress."

"Who was the girl?"

She avoided eye contact. Her voice wavered, and her knuckles were white on the steering wheel. "There was no girl, Aiden. Your mother was hallucinating. She said the girl's shawl had become entangled in one of the branches." She was crying, looking straight ahead. As we drove through the rotary by Holy Name Church, she barely missed hitting a van in the lane to our left. The man honked several times.

"Fuck you!" She rolled down her window and gave him the finger.

I began to laugh, a bit uncontrollably. I suppose it was the stress of the situation.

"What's so funny?" She glanced at me.

"You."

She laughed, too, then reached out with her right hand to grab mine. "I don't know what I would've done if your mother was hurt badly."

"But she wasn't, Nana. Don't think about it."

"You're right." She exhaled deeply.

We drove in silence. People walked in and out of stores on both sides of the street. An old lady bent over to pick up dog poop.

"Aiden, do you believe some people can see the past?"

"What?"

She moved forward in her seat and adjusted her hands on the wheel. "I think you know what I mean." She glanced at me. "Are people truly psychic? You said you think your mother's visions might be true. How can you be so sure?"

"A feeling."

"And are *you* psychic?"

"Maybe."

"You're holding back." We stopped to let a mother with a baby carriage cross.

"It's not easy to explain, Nana."

"I'm a silly old woman. I'm sure it's a coincidence."

"What is?"

"Nothing. A memory is all. From long ago and far away."

Rita was frying bologna when Martin and I arrived on Monday.

"Grab the mustard from the fridge." She used a knife to cut a dollop of butter off the stick. It sizzled in the pan, and the bologna smelled delicious. My mouth watered.

"The two of you look hungry." Her lipstick was a brownish tint. She was wearing a blouse with a brocade design of a lake and purple bell-bottom pants. "A new fashion" she would say, when she saw Martin and I giggling at her outfits. Her forehead perspired, and she daubed it with a paper towel. Several gold bracelets jingled on her arm.

She looked past us, down the dark hallway toward the front door. "Margie is always late."

"It's 'cause she never goes anywhere," Martin said. "Probably takes her a while to get out of that chair." He laughed.

"That's true. Suffers from a broken heart, but I wish she'd get over it. Arthur was the love of her life."

"Who?"

"I told you the story, Martin," I said. "Remember her high school sweetheart?"

"Oh yeah. The guy that dumped her when she got fat."

"How was your time with your ma?" Rita said.

Martin and I exchanged glances. He nodded for me to tell her.

"It didn't go so well."

She used a fork to place a piece of sizzling bologna on a plate next to the stove, then pulled the meat off the tines. Wiping more sweat off her forehead, she turned to face us. "What happened?"

"She fell from a tree and broke her arm."

The skin around her eyes tightened. "What was she doing in a tree?" She turned the burner off and brought the meat to the table. "It's self-serve," she said, motioning to the bread, mustard, and bologna.

Martin said, "She was helping a girl get down."

"Who was the girl, and what was she doing in your grandmother's tree?" She laughed.

"There was no girl," I said. "Not a *real* girl. A vision. She said the girl was wearing a green pinafore. Her scarf was caught on a branch."

"What the Christ are you talking about?" She looked at our faces.

"She *thought* she saw a girl." My jaw trembled as I made sandwiches for Martin and me, then passed the plate of bologna to Rita.

She turned to Martin, who was staring at her gold barrette.

"Do I have something in my hair?" Rita touched her head.

"I like how that metal thing glimmers."

"Thank you."

"I think the girl was a ghost," I said.

Rita frowned and sighed. "Where is your mother now?"

"She's back at McCall Hospital."

"And what about her arm?"

"It's with her too." Martin laughed.

"Stop being a wiseass, or I'll poke you with this fork." Rita raised it in the air.

"Nana says it was a hairline fracture. Mom has a cast, but she'll be OK." I bit into my sandwich.

"Catherine must be at her wits' end."

The doorbell rang. Rita stood. "Not a word about your mother's fall to Margie. She doesn't know when to keep her mouth shut. She might say something uncharitable to your grandmother." Rita walked to the front door.

"She wears the craziest clothes," Martin said.

We heard Rita say, "You shouldn't live holed up like you do. You're not a mole."

"I like moles." Margie laughed. "Got a few in my yard."

Rita and Margie entered.

"You boys look like you're up to something." Margie frowned and placed her handbag on the table. Rita moved it to a counter.

"Sit down, Margie." Rita pulled a chair out. "We're having bologna sandwiches. Help yourself."

"Fancy schmancy." Margie plopped onto the seat. Her bum hung over the edge. She wore white spandex and a red sweater over a blue T-shirt. Why do fat people always wear sweaters?

I made her a sandwich.

Rita announced, "So what are we going to do?"

"I'm nervous that we'll get in trouble. I gotta pee. Be right back." Margie got up.

When she returned, she said, "Sorry about that. Good thing they came up with adult diapers. I wear them all the time. Seems I always got to pee. When I get nervous. If I sneeze or laugh. Even when I fart."

Martin put his sandwich down. "That's appetizing."

"Honey, it's a fact of life. Older people lose control of their bladders. I saw on TV that astronauts wear MAGs during liftoff and landing."

"What are MAGs?" I said.

"Maximum absorbency garments. Something to do with gravity makes the astronauts have to go. I have a whole different perspective of John Glenn. Can't seem to get the diapers out of my mind when I look at him."

Rita tapped the end of her knife on the table. "We're not here to talk about urination and the United States space program."

"*Urination.*" Margie smirked. "Rita, you make everything sound so intellectual. The way I figure is we all shit and pee. Nothin' to be ashamed of." She took a bite of her sandwich. Mustard smeared on her chin. Rita scrubbed the frying pan in the sink.

"And women, Aiden." She tilted her head in Rita's direction. "Their bladders drop after a certain age. I bet hers has plunged," she whispered.

"What? They fall out of their you-know-what?" Martin laughed.

"Wouldn't that be funny?" She pointed at the white linoleum. "Lady, your bladder's on the floor. Watch your step." She slapped her thighs. Her bum wiggled.

"Enough!" Rita's face was pink. "Let's discuss how to get Laura home."

"We can bring her down the back stairwell. Rita, you wait in the car so we can make a quick getaway. We'll go in," Martin said.

"What about the security guard who sits by the door?" I said.

"That guy loves hearing stories about buses and the MBTA. I told him Dad worked for the T last time we were there, and he ate it up. I'll distract him."

We finished discussing our ideas. Rita said she would speak with my father to ask if Mom could stay with him until we convinced my grandmother we did the right thing.

After the sandwiches, we ate hot fudge sundaes, and Margie told more stories about the *Phil Donahue Show,* including an episode about homosexuality.

Martin watched my expression while Margie described the "homos."

We finished dessert; Rita brought us to the front door and waved when we reached the sidewalk.

I was still getting used to the layout of Boston Latin School. On my way to phys ed, I asked one of the hall monitors, a man in his midtwenties, the location of the nearest bathroom. He wore a dark gray blazer with a name tag that read "Mr. Woodlake."

I interrupted his looking at an old-fashioned timepiece hanging by a chain from his belt. His hair was slicked back in the style of the 50s, and his narrow face and pointy nose were overpowered by tortoiseshell glasses that slipped down the bridge of his nose.

"This thing doesn't work." He shook the locket. "It was a gift from my students. I'm frozen in time." He laughed. "How can I help you?" He pushed his glasses upward.

"Where's the closest restroom?"

He squinted. "You look like Martin's brother."

"I am."

"He's a great swimmer, but sometimes he doesn't know when to let up. Tell him he needs to work on his pacing. He's going to tire himself out . . . The lavatories are on the north corners of each floor." He pointed down the hall. "Around that corner. Hurry up. It's time for class."

I noticed his watch read 12:07, then hurried to the bathroom. When I came out of the stall, my grandfather was leaning against one of the sinks. "Surprised to see me here, aren't you, son?"

I was glad we were the only ones in the restroom. "I thought you only visited at night."

"Aiden, I'm with you all the time. We leave, but we stay."

"I don't get it." I washed and dried my hands.

"Someday you will."

"I'm gonna be late." I looked toward the door, hoping no one would enter.

"It may not work, but don't give up trying."

He was wearing a black suit with a white shirt and a green-and-orange tie. He seemed almost real. I had the urge to touch him.

"What may not work?" I said.

"The plan to rescue your mother. You must convince your grandmother to have your mother released into her custody. That's the only way."

"But . . ."

He disappeared. I was about to say she'd never agree. I ran down the stairs toward the gym.

I was thankful that one of the options we had for our phys ed class was lifting weights. The dark room across from the gymnasium was a hangout for those who hated sports. During any given class, there were usually five or so students pretending to work out. Hope Gallagher smiled when I entered.

"Hi, Aiden. Join the rest of us losers."

The other two girls, a chubby brunette with mottled thighs doing leg presses and a Chinese girl sitting in the corner reading *Wuthering Heights*, looked at me. I thought the skinny boy working on his biceps was sad or high. He didn't look up. Mostly, he sat there, examining his fingernails as if they were abnormal growths. The lights flickered, making our skin appear gray. The ugliness of the weight machine, a stainless-steel contraption with cables, weights, and black padded benches, depressed me. I shivered.

"You cold?" Hope said.

"Sort of." She took two cigarettes and a purple Bic lighter out of her gym shorts. "You want one?" she said before lighting up.

"No, thanks."

"Suit yourself. I shouldn't smoke either. My mother died last year of lung cancer." She placed the other cigarette back in her pocket.

"I'm sorry."

"Life sucks," she said.

The girl reading *Wuthering Heights* announced, "The fire alarm might go off."

Hope looked at the ceiling. "What fire alarm? This shithole room doesn't have one, and if it did, it probably wouldn't work. Look at these sucky lights. I feel like I'm in a prison cell.

"What's your story?" She puffed smoke in my face.

"What do you mean?"

"Are you gay?"

I blushed.

"Thought so. You shouldn't be ashamed. My uncle is gay. I love him more than anyone."

"Is he happy?"

"Sure is. He's lives with an attorney in Connecticut, a nice guy named Thomas." She exhaled. "You have pretty blue eyes." She smoothed my brows. "My mother always said you could tell gay guys by their eyes. She said they were the nicest men. She was right."

"What do you mean?"

"My father left her when she got sick. He couldn't handle my mother's illness. That's when my uncle moved in. When my mother died, he became my guardian."

"Your mother loves you," I said, sensing that her hard exterior was a way to hide pain.

"How would you know?" She laughed.

"Because she's always with you."

"What? You mean like her holding a special place in my heart even though she's rotting underground? Why do people say shit like that?"

"No. I mean *really* with you. I've seen her."

"Are you fucked up like pothead over there?" She nodded in the guy's direction. "What have you been smoking?"

"Your mother's tall, with long blonde hair and green eyes. She has a mole on her left cheek."

Her face whitened, and she rubbed the bottom of her nose. "How did you know that?"

The others weren't paying attention, except for the Chinese girl, who moved to sit on a wooden crate near us. She looked down at the novel in her lap, but I could tell she wanted to say something.

"I saw her that first day of gym class. She was smiling, and she seemed happy. She was also standing beside you on the bus and in homeroom."

"It's true," the Chinese girl said. She ran her fingers through her shiny black bangs. "Ghosts exist. In my family, we celebrate Hungry Ghost Festival."

"You've been smoking weed too," Hope said. She regained composure and feigned an I-don't-give-a-fuck attitude.

"I don't do drugs," the girl said. "We burn incense on that day and cook lots of food. Sometimes we make miniature boats and lanterns, then place them on a river or lake. The lanterns fly high into the sky. It's so beautiful." She smiled, revealing braces.

"I don't believe in ghosts. When you're dead, you're dead. That's it. Our body mixes with the earth."

The guy examining his nails looked over. "And your nails and hair keep growing."

The chubby brunette rushed out of the room.

"Guess all this talk scared her," Hope said. "You know what I think, Aiden? I think you might be able to read minds. Maybe you can see the memory of my mother. ESP is something I can believe in. But ghosts, no way."

The Chinese girl went back to reading. I wondered if she had passed the chapter in the novel when Mr. Lockwood sees Catherine's face in the window of Thrushcross Grange.

That was one of the last times Hope spoke with me. She avoided me whenever possible. I think it was the sight of me in front of the school a few weeks later that made her hurry into the street, the last time I saw her alive.

Chapter Nine

"What did my father say when you called him about what we wanted to do?"

"He was reluctant, but I convinced him it was the right thing to do. Your father's going to assist us."

I looked out my grandmother's kitchen window, twisting the phone cord. Above the shed, one of the branches of a tree had broken; its leaves were blackened.

"Brian said he'd let your mother stay with him until we convince Catherine that your mother is stable."

"I'm glad Dad's going to help us kidnap her."

Rita laughed. "Don't call it kidnapping, Aiden. We're simply allowing your mother to be with her children." A squirrel hopped onto a bushy broad-leaf shrub with red berries.

We went over the plan a bit more, including how Martin would introduce my father to the security guard who loved to talk about the MBTA, trains, and buses. We prayed that everything would work out.

For dinner that evening, Nana and I ate hot dogs and baked beans. We talked about school. I told her about Hope and how her mother died from lung cancer. I begged her to stop smoking.

"I'm not going to change. I'm too set in my ways," she said.

My grandfather visited that night.

"Why do I see ghosts?"

"Some people are chosen to encourage faith in God. You are one of many. People's biggest fear is death. They need to know there is something afterward. Many are blind, but you have the gift of sight."

"Why do I see only *certain* ghosts?"

"When a ghost appears to you, there may be a personal connection."

"Why would the mother of that girl Hope appear to me?"

"Maybe someday you'll figure it out. Existence is God's novel, with themes and symbols, like any book. Each one of us plays an important part in His tale. We are all one in the body of Christ, a character in God's story."

"What is Jesus like?"

"He's indescribable. Some things can't be explained. You will know more when you join eternal life."

My grandfather left. I tossed and turned. My mind raced. What did it all mean? Trying to comprehend the purpose of life was a big task for my young self. I am now fifty-four, and I still don't understand. I know only this: a search for understanding is the fulcrum of faith.

After a bit, I turned on the lamp and opened the drawer of my bedside table. Randomly, I turned to a page in the gospel of John: "What I do thou knowest not now; but thou shalt know hereafter."

About a month later, after we had coordinated our scheme, we drove to McCall's. Rita said it was best not to tell my mother ahead of time; she might inadvertently let on that something was up. Dad would meet us there. Rita, Margie, Martin, and I drove in Rita's red Cadillac, Martin and I in the back seat.

The day was brisk. Leaves had begun to explode into their autumnal brilliance—vivid shades of red, orange, and yellow. Through the open car windows, the scent of dying leaves wafted into the small space of our car. The lyrics of Chicago's "If You Leave Me Now" played on the radio. The lines about love being hard to find and the regret of it slipping away resonated with me. For most of the ride, we were silent. I suppose we were anxious about what we were about to attempt. Would my mother go along with the escape? Would it actually work? If we succeeded in helping her escape, then what? I had no doubt we were doing the right thing, but I was unsure of what to do afterward.

When we drove up the curvy road to the admissions building, we saw my father's blue Volkswagen Golf. He was leaning against the trunk. He crossed and uncrossed his arms, looking around as if a SWAT team lurked in the branches of the pastoral landscape or lay on the rooftops of the buildings, peering every so often to watch our actions.

"Don't look so nervous," Rita said, getting out of the car. Martin and I opened our doors, but she told us to stay put. Margie hummed along to the radio, patting Arthur, who lay in her lap.

"Are you sure we're doing the right thing?" my father said to Rita. "Catherine is going to be mad as hell."

"Forget about that. I know how to handle her. She'll be OK in the end . . . Follow my car. I'll let all of you go in and do as we discussed. I'll pull my car near the back door of the building."

We listened intently.

"Everything will be all right. Won't it, boys?"

"Dad, we got nothing to worry about. Remember, we're Glencars!" Martin patted his chest. "We can do anything."

Margie kissed Arthur, then spat his cat hairs onto the car seat, picking some off her chin and twirling them between her fingers.

As we approached my mother's building, my stomach grumbled.

"You hungry?" Martin said. "I can grab some of that applesauce they store in the kitchen refrigerator."

"Nervous."

"Don't be nervous, Aiden. Nothing bad's gonna happen."

The four of us—my father, Margie, Martin, and I (and Arthur, of course)—checked in at the nurses' station.

The receptionist, a college-age girl with purple nails and feather earrings, said, "Can I help you?" She looked at the cat and sneezed. "Sorry, I'm allergic."

Nurse Nancy approached us. "Animals are not allowed on the floor. Hospital rules." Other nurses, doctors, and aides walked up and down the hallways. Beside the nurses' station, a woman restrained in what looked like an adult-size baby chair repeated "Oyayaya, oyyayaya" again and again. One of the aides wiped her mouth on her bib. A janitor emptied a wastebasket into a large bin on rollers.

"Arthur is a service cat. I have agoraphobia. Without him, I'd never leave the house." Margie cried. She was a good actress. I was beginning to think my grandmother and her friends should win an Emmy or two. "I can show you my doctor's note."

Nurse Nancy wrinkled her nose and averted her gaze. "That won't be necessary."

"We're here to see my wife, Laura Glencar," my father said.

"Wait here while I check on her."

A few moments later, Nancy waved for us to come down the hallway. Arthur hadn't scratched anyone or caused a scene. One of our distraction ideas had failed.

My mother sat on her bed, putting blush on her face. Her roommate (I assumed it was her new friend Nell) said hello from behind the curtain that divided the room. Her voice sounded familiar.

"Hi," I answered. The others, excited and focused on my mother, ignored her.

My mother extended her arms. "Come here, boys."

Her hug was warm. She kissed Martin's and my cheeks. Her red blouse smelled like roses.

"You even brought Arthur." She laughed, looking past us. "How are you, Margie? It's been a long time."

"I'm alive."

Mom's cheeks blushed slightly. "Hi, Brian," she said to my father. He was dressed in his work uniform—black pants and the light blue shirt with the *T* insignia.

He smiled, unfolding his arms. "You look great."

My mother said, "You do. I love that color on you."

"Shit! Where is Arthur?" Margie said. "Laura, can I go behind the curtain to look for him?"

"Of course. There's no one behind there. Just an empty bed." My mother laughed.

"Very funny, Laura," the woman said.

Margie said, "Gosh darn it! He peed on the pillow."

"Raindrops keep falling on my head," the woman sang, humming the rest of the song, every once in a while saying "ooh aah" as if she were her own backup singer. Again, I tried to think when I'd heard that voice.

My father pulled out the blue chair for Margie, who returned with Arthur. "Sit, Margie. I'm going to use the restroom"

"There's one right behind you." My mother pointed.

My father looked at Martin and me. "That's OK. I saw a restroom by the entrance. I'll give you guys time to talk." He winked. "Martin told me that the security guard wanted some information about working for the MBTA. He promised the guy I'd chat with him."

When he left, my mother said, "He gets uncomfortable in hospitals. He probably thought he'd see a bedpan in the bathroom." She laughed.

"Shouldn't we call someone to clean up the pee?" Margie said.

"It's OK," my mother said. "I'll tell the nurse when she comes back."

"I already wiped it up," the lady said.

Margie sighed. "I'm so sorry, Laura." She petted Arthur. His hairs floated in the air. She squeezed him and bent close to his face.

"Why did you pee?" She looked at us. "He must get nervous like me."

I whispered to my mother, "We're getting you out of here."

She stood. "Great. I'm sick of this place." She emptied her bedside table and closet, putting her things into the red suitcase Martin had lifted onto the bed.

When he clicked it shut, he said, "It's time. Walk slowly out of the room. Find Dad. Act real casual. Pretend you're showing them around, Mom."

As we exited the room, Margie said, "I'm so anxious. My feet are sweating."

Dad had managed to move the young security guy away from his post at the rear exit. The light above the doorway flashed.

I whispered to my mother, "What does that mean?"

"Means they'll think I'm dying. Martin must have pulled the call light out of the wall."

Three nurses ran into my mother's room, almost crashing into Margie and Arthur. The security guard said something into the radio, then hurried toward the commotion. Dad opened the exit door. "Quick."

Martin took howling Arthur from Margie so she could hold on to the stairwell bannister. Drips of urine pattered his legs. "Gross," he said.

Dad raced down the stairs and held open the door to outside. My mother's laugh was infectious. Our laughter echoed in the cold stairwell; Arthur's howls grew louder. Margie moaned, easing her fat body down the stairs as rapidly as she could. I called to her, "Hold the railing. You don't want to fall."

Mom raised her cast. "You'll end up with one of these things."

"I don't think they have one for broken asses." Margie breathed heavily. I prayed she wouldn't have a heart attack.

When we were outside, Rita honked her horn. All the doors of her car were open. We hurried across the lawn.

"Don't drop the cat," my father said to Martin. "Get in the car. Fast."

Another security guard and Nurse Nancy bolted around the corner of the building and stood between the five of us and the car. "You can't leave." She held her hand up like a crossing guard. "Grab Ms. Glencar," she said to the security guard. His shirt was wet under his arms, and his pale belly was visible between buttons.

My mother said, "OK. OK. We wanted to go outside for a bit." She glanced up. "Isn't the sky lovely? And look at that dove in the tree."

"Dove?" The heavy security guard stared at the maple. My mother kicked his shin.

"Fuck. That hurt." He hopped, holding his leg.

"Not as much as staying in this hellhole," my mother said. She escaped his grasp and was almost seated in the back of the car when a black sedan with two additional guards blocked Rita in.

"Lady, you're not going anywhere," one shouted from his window.

"She's got a name," my father said, spit flying from his mouth. "It's Ms. Glencar. Ms. Laura Glencar."

The ward security guard spoke calmly to my father. "Sir, I understand you want your wife to go home. But we have procedures to follow. You have rules at your work. You were telling me what happens when someone jumps the tracks."

My father's face slackened, and his shoulders fell. Rita got out of the car. "Why can't the young woman go home?" she said to Nurse Nancy. "The children need their mother." She was wearing a black pantsuit with a beret, as if she were a sleuth in a spy thriller.

Nancy walked over to my mother and whispered in her ear, guiding her toward the entryway of the building.

"It will be all right," Mom said to us. "Go home. Visit again soon." She tried to sound cheery, but I felt her sadness.

She waved before entering, Nurse Nancy holding the door. The young security guard said he was sorry to my father and walked toward the rear entrance. Margie, my father, Rita, Martin, and I exchanged glances. Then we heard a cooing sound. On a tree branch, a light gray-brown mourning dove fluttered its wings. Beyond the tree, on the lawn, I saw my grandfather. He waved to me. I waved back.

Margie said, "Who you waving to?"

"The dove."

"You're fucked up." Martin laughed.

"Watch your language," my father said. He followed my eyes to the lawn beyond.

Margie took Arthur from Martin. "I'm exhausted. I gotta get in the car . . . You were bad today," she said to Arthur, rubbing her nose against his. Rita stood silently, her eyes watery, looking at my father, Martin, and me.

Dad crouched and wrapped his arms around the both of us. "Don't worry, boys. Everything will be OK."

Chapter Ten

Rita and Margie drove together. My father took Martin and me in his car. Martin looked out the window to avoid my eyes. I think he was crying. Occasionally, I saw my father watching the both of us in the rearview mirror. I felt a pit in my stomach, anticipating my grandmother's reaction. Nurse Nancy would certainly call her.

When we all had pulled in the driveway, Rita said, "Let me do the talking."

My father had to be at work, so he couldn't stay. Rita said she would see that Martin got to Aunt Clara's later.

My grandmother was sitting on the couch, pretending to read the newspaper.

"We're sorry, Catherine."

She didn't look up. Her lips were tight, and her eyes were red from crying.

"The boys want their mother home."

Martin and I sat in two wingback chairs on the other side of the room. Margie went to the bathroom. Rita stood in front of the glass-topped coffee table that separated her from my grandmother. "Won't you say something?"

She folded the newspaper and threw it at Rita. "You think I don't want Laura home? That I'm a mean old bitch who loves that her daughter is in a nuthouse?" Her fists were clenched. "You always have to be the heroine, Rita. The *kind* one, the *nicest* person." She snickered.

"That's uncalled for, Catherine. I was trying to help."

My grandmother threw up her hands and sat on the couch. She rolled her eyes. "Yes, Rita. You're always trying to help." She sighed.

Martin and I exchanged glances.

Nana continued, inhaling on a cigarette. "I love my daughter. And I hate that she needs to be in that God-awful place."

Rita circled the coffee table and tried to hug her. My grandmother pushed her arms away. Rita stumbled, knocking the glass top onto the floor. It broke into pieces.

"Grandpa wants Mom to come home," I blurted. They looked at me.

"What are you saying, Aiden?" my grandmother said.

"He told me."

Martin stared and shook his head.

"That's impossible. He's dead." Nana extended her arms along the top of the couch. Martin moved closer to me.

"He visits."

"What in the hell are you talking about?" my grandmother said.

"Sometimes he comes to me at night."

"Aiden, lots of people have dreams about people they've lost," she said.

"Nana, Grandpa wanted me to tell you it wasn't your fault that he died."

"Of course it wasn't my fault." She puffed on the cigarette, eyeing me suspiciously.

"Then why do you cry at night and ask God for forgiveness? Grandpa says he's in the bedroom with you. He told me to tell you he was 'full as a bingo bus' that night. He's sorry."

Martin laughed. "What's that? A bunch of old people on their way to play bingo in a church basement?"

Nana's face whitened, and she tapped her cigarette on the ashtray. "Where did you hear that expression?"

"What does it mean?" Martin said.

"It's an Irish saying for drunk," Rita said.

"You would know," my grandmother said, looking past her.

"He told me that you should stop blaming yourself for leaving him in the chair when you went to bed. It's not your fault that he choked on his vomit."

"That's gross," Martin said.

Margie entered, wiping her hands on her pants. She sat on the love seat.

My grandmother shook, tears on her face. "Your grandfather and I had been arguing. He was drunk. I left him in the chair. I should have made him come with me."

Rita sat next to her.

"Rita wouldn't have left him. She would have done the right thing. Taken him to bed with her," she said to the rest of us.

"What's that supposed to mean?" Rita said.

"You know exactly what it means." Her voice was low and firm.

"You kids should probably go upstairs," Margie said. Her leg jiggled.

"They're old enough to hear what I have to say, Margaret."

"And what is that?" Rita stared, her face rigid.

My grandmother paused and spoke calmly. "That you're a whore. And you sleep with married men." She inhaled and blew smoke. "I'm sure Sean thought you were a good fuck."

Margie stood, her legs wobbly. "Oh my God! Boys, you really need to go play or somethin'."

Martin pulled me from the couch and guided me upstairs.

When we were seated on my bed, he said, "Well, that was a nice end to the day."

We both laughed, then sat quietly for a bit, staring into space.

"Do you think I'm crazy, Martin?"

"How so?"

"What I said about Grandpa."

He put his arm over my shoulder. "Nothing crazy about you, brother. I believe you."

"I don't want to be put away like Mom."

"Listen to me." He held my face. "If you say Grandpa visits you, then Grandpa fuckin' visits you. If anyone has a problem with that, they got me to deal with . . . Remember what I always say?"

"'I will always have your back,'" I answered.

"Don't ever forget that."

After that day, my grandmother looked at me differently. Fear? Did she think I was schizophrenic like my mother?

One evening, she sat on the living room couch and looked through an old photo album.

"How did you know those details about your grandfather's death? I told everyone he had a heart attack because I wanted to protect his reputation." Her words slurred, and she held a glass of whiskey.

"I told you, Nana."

She closed the album. "Stop with your malarkey. Ghosts don't exist." She touched her throat; it had begun to redden.

I sat next to her.

"What does he look like?" she said.

"He has dark curly hair and thick black-framed glasses."

She puffed on her cigarette. "You've seen photographs . . . What else has he told you?"

"He said Mom has second sight like your mother, who fell down a well."

Her leg trembled against mine. She turned away. "Go to your room. I can't talk about this any longer."

"Nana, don't be mad."

"I'm not mad, Aiden. Just confused." She rubbed her temples. Then she picked up the album, preoccupied with a photo about halfway through the pages.

"I'm confused too." I walked toward the stairs.

Lost in thought, she didn't hear me.

Nana had left for work by the time I was dressed and ready for school. I ate strawberry Pop-Tarts and made myself a cup of tea. I had fifteen minutes before I needed to catch the bus. I went to the couch and opened the frayed black cover of the photo album. The pages were filled with old black and whites of Nana's family in Ireland. When I reached the halfway mark, I scrutinized the images. When Nana examined the photos, she appeared sad and anxious. Why would some old pictures have that effect?

Pasted to a faded black page was a paper written in longhand. Someone, I suppose my grandmother, had copied a poem by William Butler Yeats—"The Lake Isle of Innisfree."

I will arise and go now, and go to Innisfree,
And a small cabin build there, of clay and wattles made;
Nine bean-rows will I have there, a hive for the honey-bee,
And live alone in the bee-loud glade.

And I shall have some peace there, for peace comes dropping slow,
Dropping from the veils of the morning to where the cricket sings;
There midnight's all a glimmer, and noon a purple glow,
And evening full of the linnet's wings.

I will arise and go now, for always night and day
I hear lake water lapping with low sounds by the shore;
While I stand on the roadway, or on the pavements grey,
I hear it in the deep heart's core.

Underneath her cursive and continuing onto the next page were five photographs, yellowed with age. She had written "Our Trip to

Innisfree" above the series of photos. Three girls and a boy, my grandmother and her siblings, sat in a small rowboat on a lake. The boy, tall and skinny, wore suspenders and a scally cap, his shirt buttoned to the top of its round collar. He grinned as he held one of the oars above his head. The girls, who appeared to be in their early teens, one perhaps younger, were dressed in old-fashioned long dresses. They were laughing at something he'd said. I spotted my grandmother immediately. She was at the back of the boat, looking toward the island beyond, half her face visible, a shawl over her head. In each photograph, the island appeared closer. The boy was rowing in the latter pictures; only the backs of the girls' heads were visible, hair cut short, thick locks curling inward. In one picture, my grandmother draped her hand into the water.

In the final picture, my grandmother was halfway up a pine tree, her shawl caught on a branch. Her brother, looking alarmed, reached for her. Her panicked face was obvious as he grabbed for her legs. She clutched the branch, which had entangled her shawl.

So that was a pinafore dress, I thought. Because the photograph was black and white, I couldn't make out the color, but it could have been green. My forehead was perspiring. I slammed the album shut, grabbed my backpack, and ran to the bus stop. My mother had seen my grandmother in the pine tree on the day she fell and broke her arm.

During the ride to school, I looked at people and houses outside the bus, but mostly I was lost in thought. Grandpa said that all time happens at once. Could my mother truly have seen Nana in the tree? Was she trying to save her child-mother in Ireland? "There is no true

division between past and future; there is rather a single existence,"
my grandfather had said. As I exited the bus, I imagined my future
self, alive and well in another dimension. What was my older self
thinking now? Could he see me getting off the bus? Where had life
brought him?

"Hey, watch it," said a girl with heavy eyeliner and black eye
shadow.

"I'm sorry."

"Pay attention."

"I was preoccupied."

"Fuck off, freak. Preoccupied." She laughed.

The wheels of a bus screeched. Girls screamed. I turned and saw
a bus hit Hope. She bounced onto a white Chrysler in the opposite
lane. Her limp body rolled off the hood onto the street. All traffic
stopped.

"Call nine-one-one," one of the football players yelled, rushing
toward her. At the curb, girls cried, and boys said "Fuck!" and other
curse phrases. The bus driver, an older black man, ran to Hope. The
owner of the Chrysler, a businessman in a gray suit, tears on his face,
flailed his arms and yelled, "It was an accident. She came out of
nowhere."

Soon Principal Castellanos and the assistant principal, a hand
over her mouth, rushed to the street. Security guards hollered that all
students should immediately go to class. Before I passed out, Hope's
mother, a look of joy on her face, grabbed her spirit daughter. They
rose from the bloody pavement, abandoning her mangled body.
Hugging, they ascended into the sky.

I awoke in the school nurse's office. She had placed an ammonia inhalant under my nose.

"How do you feel?" she said. She smelled like garlic.

"Shitty."

She laughed, aiming a small flashlight into my eyes. "Your pupils look OK. Sit up slowly."

She felt the back of my head. "You have a small bump." She rested her hands in her lap. "Does your head hurt?"

"A little."

"Do you feel nauseous?"

"No."

I felt tears on my face and wiped them away.

She smiled and handed me Kleenex. "Aiden, I know this is hard for you. What you saw was horrific. But Hope died immediately. She suffered no pain. Sit here while I call your mother."

"My grandmother."

She looked at me quizzically.

"I live with my grandmother."

"OK. I'll check your records and call her."

A few moments later, she returned. "Your grandmother is on her way. I told her she should bring you to the emergency ward." She laughed. "She's a clever and stubborn woman. Said she was a nurse and asked me about your condition. She wanted to know every detail. She determined that a hospital visit was 'unwarranted.'"

"I don't have to go to the hospital?"

"No, dear. I don't think you have anything to worry about. Your grandmother knows how to take care of you." She propped a pillow at the top of the examining couch and told me to lie back. Then she laid a thin blanket on me and told me to rest. "Call me if your headache gets worse or you feel sick. I will be right outside this room." She dimmed the light before softly closing the door.

About an hour later, my grandmother and I were in her car headed home. I slept most of the way. Periodically, she tapped my shoulder. "Are you OK, Aiden?"

"Yes," I said irritably. I was in the thick of dreams. I was at the beach with my mother. Then I was at a graveyard underneath an ancient oak tree. Aunt Clara stood next to me. Someone's casket was being lifted into a hole. I dove into the hole and found myself swimming in the ocean, the beach far in the distance. Martin swam toward me; my mother watched us from the shore. Someone called, "Come away, O human child, to the waters and the wild."

When we arrived home, my grandmother shook me awake. "Do you think you can stand on your own?"

"Yes. I feel like I'm in a dream."

"We're all in a dream, Aiden. 'We are such stuff as dreams are made on, and our life is rounded with a sleep.' Your grandfather loved that quote. I think there's a wisdom to it. You need a nap." She opened the car door for me. As I got up, she put her arm around my torso. "Walk slowly. We're almost inside."

"We're almost inside," I repeated. "That makes sense. I understand."

"Aiden, you're confused. You'll feel better once you've slept."

I stopped halfway across the lawn and looked up at her. "I'm not confused, Nana."

She kissed my cheek and pulled me forward.

After two nights of disturbing dreams, I was relieved to wake to a bright Sunday.

My grandmother was on the phone in the kitchen. She put her hand over the mouthpiece and told me to eat before the eggs and bacon got cold.

"There's nothing abnormal about him. I think *you're* abnormal. What type of woman changes her name and puts on such airs? 'Clarise.' No one believes for even an instant that you're French." She humphed.

My grandmother snickered as she listened to Aunt Clara's response. "You've got the face of an Irish maid. Pug nose, freckles, and tiny lips. You should be serving the sparkling wine, not drinking it." She mouthed "bitch" to me and rolled her eyes as she continued to listen.

"We have already discussed this. *I* believe him. And Martin is smart enough to make up his own mind. Nothing fazes him. He accepts everyone and most certainly his brother."

"Herself hung up on me."

"Why does she think I'm abnormal."

"Because she's as smart as a cabbage." She joined me at the table, smoking and drinking her coffee. "Ignore her, Aiden. She's an arse."

"What did she say?"

She tamped her cigarette in an ashtray. "Evidently, your brother thinks you're some New-Age psychic. He has the notion that the two of you should go into business. He wants you to be a medium."

I laughed.

"I'll speak with him. Martin's off his nut."

"He's not crazy. He probably thinks it's cool that I see ghosts."

She was silent, sipping her coffee, holding the mug close to her mouth and staring off into space.

"What are you thinking about?"

"I'm perplexed about all this. Might you just have a creative bent like your mother? All that art she makes requires imagination." She got up and put her mug in the sink. She braced her hands against the counter. "I'm frightened for you." Her back and arms trembled. "And you must feel awful about your friend."

"I'll be OK. Hope's with her mother now. She's happy. Grandpa says eternal life is wonderful."

She kneeled by my chair and reached for my hand. "Aiden, this spirit of your grandfather. Maybe it's not really him. There are evil ghosts. He could be trying to fool you."

"Then how does he know so much about you?"

She bent her head. "I don't know. I just want the Good Shepherd to protect you."

I placed my hand on her shoulder. "Don't worry, Nana. Everything will be OK."

"You'll be going to your friend's wake and funeral, won't you?"

"I don't like wakes or funerals. Besides, I hardly knew her. What good are wakes anyway?"

Her eyes widened. "To pay respect to the family, Aiden."

"I don't want to go, Nana," I said loudly.

"Can't make ya." She sighed. "Tell you what, you say an extra prayer for her at church today. We must always pray for the departed." She squeezed my hand and stood. "Get dressed. Wear something nice. I'll pray for your friend while I wait."

Chapter Eleven

"Do you think Mom drinking from the chalice worked?"

"God works in mysterious ways. I don't know that a sip of wine from that glorious cup performed a miracle if that's what you mean. But I have hope." Nana wiped her hands on her apron and put it in a drawer. "I'm not sure that I believe in miracles in the usual sense. Every moment is a miracle, don't you think?"

"Yes."

She threw my crumpled napkins into the wastebasket. "We make our own miracles. There's a saying from the old country: 'It's the good horse that draws its own cart.' The thing is we must make things happen on our own instead of sitting on our arses waiting for Jesus to put the world right." She smiled and motioned for me to get up from my chair. "That's why we'll do what is required. Get yourself ready for church."

In less than an hour, we were in Mission Hill. My grandmother had the hardest time parallel parking.

"Get out," she said.

I stood on the sidewalk and shouted, "Stop. You're gonna hit that car."

She bent over the seat and looked at me through the passenger window. "How much room do I have?"

"About two inches."

"Christ." She extended her arm across the top of the seat and turned to look behind her before reversing and smashing into the red Ford Mustang.

"*Shite*." She glanced around to see if anyone was watching. There was no one in sight. Everyone was inside listening to the Mass.

After rolling up the windows and locking the car, she stood on the street opposite to where I stood on the sidewalk.

"You smashed the bumper."

"How do you know it was me? Look at the scratches along this side of the car. Obviously, this individual doesn't know how to drive."

I joined her and traced my fingers along the scratches.

"Don't do that."

"Why?"

"You'll leave fingerprints."

I laughed. "You think they're gonna dust the car for prints?"

We watched two cars pass. My grandmother smiled and waved at the drivers. "Let's get this over with." She straightened her blue dress and grabbed my hand. "Hurry and cross."

"Do you have the chalice?"

She patted her handbag. "It's inside here. I had to remove my makeup bag and a brush to make room. The sacrifices we make."

We both laughed. I opened the carved wooden door for her. She looked at the red Mustang before entering and whispered, "We've got to make this fast. Before Mass ends. I don't want a scene with the owner of that car."

The air was musty, warm, and dark. It took my eyes a few moments to adjust.

The priest said, "A reading from the first letter of Saint John . . . 'Beloved: See what love the Father has bestowed on us that we may be called the children of God. Yet so we are.'" People turned in the pews to look as we walked down the aisle. My grandmother bowed to them. "'The reason the world does not know us is that it did not know him. Beloved, we are God's children now.'" He paused and watched us climb the altar, then continued reading, eyeing us occasionally. "'What we shall be has not yet been revealed. We do know that when it is revealed we shall be like him, for we shall see him as he is.'"

My grandmother pulled me to a bench at the sidewall. We sat down. The cool stone felt good against my back. The priest stared at us. People in the congregation moved in their seats, whispering and gawking at us.

"'Everyone who has this hope based on him makes himself pure, as he is pure.'" He held up his index finger to the congregation and smiled, then walked over to us and whispered, "May I help you?"

"Yes, Father, like you were saying, that bit about 'bestowed' and 'God's children now.'"

"I don't follow you," he said. The people in the pews were talking louder.

Someone shouted, "Is everything OK, Father?"

"Yes. Yes," he called back. "I'll be right with you." Again he held up his index finger.

I pulled my grandmother's handbag from her lap and took out the chalice. "It is revealed!"

"Where did you get that?"

"A homeless man on the Boston Common was drinking beer from it. I recognized it as the chalice that was stolen. Saw that article in the *Globe*," my grandmother said.

"He was all dirty and sad looking. He smelled real bad too. I think he needed some healing," I interjected.

"We prayed with the man and asked him to let us return it," my grandmother said. "I said God would forgive him because we are all God's children and all that other palaver you were saying."

The priest's face lit up. "It's a miracle," he hollered to the congregation, holding the chalice above his head and walking to the center of the altar. "Thanks be to God."

The people repeated, "Thanks be to God."

My grandmother pulled me from the bench. "Let's get the hell out of here," she whispered.

People clapped as we hurried down the aisle.

"Wait," the priest said. "We don't know your names."

"I'm Elaine, and this is my grandson Galahad."

We ran out the door and crossed the street.

Nana's hands shook as she tried to unlock the door. "Aiden, you'll have to do it for me. I'm a nervous wreck." She handed me the keys.

An elderly gentleman with a cane yelled, "Yoo-hoo. Come back. We want to speak with you."

"Yoo-hoo," my grandmother answered, and she waved. "We'll be right over . . . Hurry up, Aiden. We've got to get in the car."

I opened her door and ran to the other side. Both of us slammed the doors hard. I thought the glass could have broken. My grandmother rolled her window down. "We're terribly sorry. We've got an emergency. My grandson is hyperventilating. He gets nervous around crowds."

On cue, I breathed hard and waved to the man. I held my chest and coughed, pretending I was near death.

The man started down the steps, holding his cane and grasping the railing.

My grandmother said, "Let's get out of here before that buttinsky falls!" We swerved into the street and sped off. "Who says 'yoo-hoo' anymore? He must be demented."

"Where'd you come up with those crazy names?" I pressed my hands against the dashboard because she was driving so fast.

"Something I read. Probably one of your grandfather's old books."

Aunt Clara wasn't happy when my grandmother and I showed up one day. Nana wanted to say a few things. She honked the horn in front of the house.

Martin ran out. My little cousins Greta and Gary followed him.

"Don't go near that car," Aunt Clara yelled from behind.

My grandmother slammed her door and walked up the bricks toward Aunt Clara.

"Why are you here?"

"I want to talk to you."

"And what do you want to talk about?"

"I don't like that you tell Martin his brother is crazy."

Martin waved to me while my cousins laughed and pulled on his legs. They managed to get him lying on the grass. Martin wrestled with them, and they pealed with delight.

"You can't keep a good man down," he said, pretending to have difficulty raising himself.

"I'm not comfortable with this paranormal business," Aunt Clara said to my grandmother. She shivered in the wind, arms folded against her chest. She was staring at me in the passenger seat as if I were possessed. "I think you should get him checked."

"Don't be so dramatic, Clara."

"It's Clarise."

"So you've told me many times. I don't like the sound of it. Besides, Clara is your baptismal name."

"I spoke with my pastor." Aunt Clara touched her neck. "He said this could be the work of a demon or even the devil. That is, if it's true. Or it could be schizophrenia."

"If Aiden says it's true, then it's true."

"How are you so sure? His mother heard voices, too, and look where she ended up."

My grandmother stepped forward. "You keep Laura out of this."

"Catherine. You're a nurse. You know that mental illness is genetic," Aunt Clara said. "He looks terrible. Dark circles under his eyes and so pale." She stared at me.

"His friend from school was run over by a car. Aiden's experiencing emotional trauma. Have some compassion. Don't they teach you that in your cult?"

Aunt Clara gasped. She ran to the car and hugged me through the open window.

"I'm sorry about your friend. He's in heaven now."

"She."

"Yes, she's in heaven now." She looked at me as though I were a bird with a broken wing.

"How do you know?" I said.

"Know what?" She scratched her temple.

"Where she is?"

She rubbed her arm. "That's where everyone goes when they die, Aiden." Her eyes blinked.

"Where is heaven?"

She pointed upward.

"I doubt it."

A man across the street tried to control his yapping Chihuahua by pulling on its leash.

"Aiden, you shouldn't doubt such things. Didn't the priest at her service say she was in heaven? He's a man of God."

"I didn't go to her service. She wouldn't have known I was there. She's dead. She lives in another dimension now. They probably have to fill out paperwork to be admitted. I bet she's waiting in a long line." I wanted to get a rise out of her.

"Paperwork?" She made eyes at my grandmother. "Aiden, there's no paperwork in heaven."

"Have you ever been there? I heard there's all these aisles, and they don't have enough help to process the dead people. Saint Peter gets irritated sometimes too."

My grandmother suppressed laughter by coughing. "You see. He's out of his head. The boy is suffering from terrible stress. He might even need medication."

I wiggled my nose and rolled my eyes from side to side.

"Just look at him," my grandmother said. "He may never be the same, poor thing."

"I'll pray for you, Aiden."

"Got any pelican pins? It will give him something to take his mind off the whole affair," my grandmother said.

"I do, as a matter of fact. I'll go get some."

When she entered the house, my grandmother floored the gas pedal. Martin, still wrestling with the kids, waved goodbye.

"You're a little *divil*. You almost made me feel bad for her."

We both laughed.

A sour smell permeated the car's interior. I felt nails scratching the back of my neck. Then a whisper in my ear: "Maybe you'll be locked up in a looney bin like your ma," Moira cackled.

I closed my eyes, hoping she would disappear. I said the "Our Father" aloud.

"It's good you're praying," my grandmother said. "You should say a "Hail Mary" while you're at it. I know Herself is annoying, but you shouldn't torment people. Do you understand?" She couldn't help bursting into a laugh.

When I finished the prayer, the smell was gone. I looked in the rearview mirror. The back seat was empty.

When we got home, the phone rang. Nana answered.

"I apologize. I thought it best to hurry home so he could nap . . . Next time Martin visits, tell him to bring the pelicans . . . Clara, I'm not going to talk about this anymore." She sighed. "I want to take *both* boys to see their mother. They need her. Can't you understand that? And they need each other."

Nana listened.

"We're all uneasy. That's the story of life."

I could hear Clara say "As God is my witness," but I missed what came after.

"Listen, Scarlett O'Hara, this isn't the Civil War, and that dump you live in looks nothing like Tara."

She hung up and looked me over. "The back of your neck is bleeding. Turn your head . . . "Why are you always scratching yourself?" She squinted. "You could get an infection."

She grabbed a paper towel from under the sink and wet it. She daubed my neck, then balled the towel and threw it in the trash.

"Maybe I should get you checked like Clara said. You've got to stop scratching yourself. Do you understand, Aiden?"

"I'll stop."

"Good. Now I need a drink." She plopped into a kitchen chair. "Pour me one, will you dear?"

"Yes, Nana."

The next weekend, my grandmother and I went to McCall's. Martin was at swim practice. Nurse Nancy smiled. "Laura is doing great. She's been busy drawing. Quite a talented artist."

"She gets that from me. I studied at the Louvre in Paris," Nana said.

"Really?" Nancy cocked her head. She led us down the hallway.

My grandmother asked, "You think I'm incapable?"

Nancy laughed. "Not at all. It was a stupid thing to say." She turned. "I didn't mean to offend you."

"No offense taken. Next time I'll carry a paintbrush."

"Here we are," Nancy said outside Mom's room. She smiled at me. "I bet you're excited to see your mother."

"We're good now. You can go," my grandmother said.

When she left, I said, "I didn't know you were an artist, Nana."

"Don't be silly, Aiden. That was blarney. Nancy Nurse is a Lady Muck. Thinks her shit doesn't stink." She pushed me forward. "Go in. Your mother will be so happy to see you."

"Hi, Mom." I hurried to her bed, where she sat drawing in her sketchpad. She wore a green gown that accentuated her eyes.

"I want to eat you up." She kissed my face and hugged me tight. "I've missed you so much. There's no one to talk with at this place." She looked past me. "Aren't you going to kiss me, Ma?"

"You need to visit with Aiden. I have to speak with the nurse. I'll be back soon."

My mother asked me about my favorite subjects in schools, my grades, my teachers, and any clubs I was involved in. "Do you have a special someone?"

"Martin said that girls are a pain in the butt. But not you, Mom."

"I understand, honey."

"Mom, I don't have a girlfriend. I have friends that are girls, but not girlfriends. Do you know what I mean?"

"Sit down, Aiden. I brought the subject up because I know what's bothering you." She put her arm around me and kissed my forehead. "Aiden, it doesn't matter who we love. Do you understand?"

I nodded.

"Grandpa visited me a few nights ago."

I felt my mouth open.

"Don't look so surprised. He was my father."

"But you never told me he visited you."

"He died when I was young, but in my teenage years, he would come to me at night, like he does with you."

"What did he say?"

"He told me I need to talk with you. Said you were being harassed by a nasty spirit."

"I'm gay, Mom."

"I know you are, sweetheart, and there is nothing wrong with that. We are all God's children."

"Do you think I'll go to hell?"

"Of course not. Hell doesn't exist."

"I don't like being gay."

"Someday you'll find a wonderful partner and be happy. I'm sure of that . . . Your grandfather told me that I needed to comfort you with hope. You need to know that things always get better."

"He wasn't talking about that type of hope. My friend from school, Hope Gallagher, was hit by a bus."

She paled. "Is she OK?"

"She's dead."

She hugged me and kissed my face several times. "How awful. Her poor mother. I can't imagine losing a child. It would destroy me."

"Her mother was there."

"That's horrific. To see your child die so violently."

"Her mother is dead."

"Aiden." She pulled back and stared at me. "You're confusing me."

"Her spirit was there. They hugged and rose into the sky . . . Their spirit selves, I mean. I saw Hope's spirit leave her body."

"Did you tell your grandmother this?" She rubbed the top of her hand and looked toward the door.

"No. Everyone thinks I'm crazy. They call me a freak at school. I keep secrets. Hope was the only kid who talked to me."

"Aiden, someday you'll have lots of friends. Adolescence is hard."

"Everyone loves Martin."

"You're different. Don't compare yourself to him."

We heard loud voices in the hall.

My grandmother said, "I'm taking her home, Nancy Nurse. And I have every right to. I'm her mother, and I was appointed guardian by the court. So mind your own business. Haven't you got a bedpan to empty?"

They entered the room.

"Let me at least call the psychiatrist."

"That won't be necessary. Nothing he says will change my mind . . . Laura, pack up your things. You're coming home."

"Give me at least a few moments to collect the paperwork, Mrs. Mulroy. You need to sign her out AMA."

"That will be fine, Nancy. I'm a nurse too. I know the procedure. Get the papers. It will give us time to get organized."

My mother and I packed her suitcases.

"I'm sorry for bringing you here," my grandmother said to Mom. "You should be home with Aiden and Martin."

When Nurse Nancy returned, my grandmother signed the necessary forms, and we left. Before getting into the car, both my mother and I saw him. My grandfather was sitting on the grass beneath the tree. He smiled and waved to us. A star shone in the twilit sky.

"Hurry up, slowpokes," my grandmother said, then turned toward the maple. "What are you looking at?" She followed our gaze.

"Hope," my mother said, laying her arm over my shoulder and guiding me into the back seat before closing my door.

When they were inside, I said, "How can you *see* hope?"

My grandmother started the car and looked at Mom. "Hope is sitting right beside me."

Mom touched the back of my grandmother's neck. The car moved forward.

My mother's sketchbook fell open. An image of a painting slid out. She had copied it in her book, using different shades of pencil. A blindfolded woman in a green gown sat atop a light brown globe, her head bent to the left. She played a lyre with a single string. In the background, one star sparkled in the gray-blue sky. Printed underneath the reproduction was "Hope, 1886, George Frederic Watts."

After a while, my grandmother said, "I've got to make a stop before we go home."

"Where?" my mother said.

"Rita's house."

"Why?" I asked.

My grandmother looked at me in the rearview mirror. "Aiden, what I said to Rita last week was cruel. I humiliated and embarrassed her. I need to apologize. Do you understand?"

"I do."

My mother kissed my grandmother's cheek and leaned against her shoulder.

I thought of Innisfree and the photographs in my grandmother's album. I rolled down my window and imagined crickets were singing. I saw the photograph of my grandmother as a panicked young girl in the tree. A brother rescued her, Martin would always rescue me, and we had rescued Mom. At this instant, people throughout the world were saving one another.

Somewhere, linnets flew through evening skies. Midnights were glimmering, peace was dropping, and the veils of morning would rise once more.

Chapter Twelve

The next Saturday evening, Margie invited us to her place to celebrate my mother's homecoming. The house was immaculate.

"Margie, I can't believe how beautiful your place looks," my grandmother said as we took off our jackets. "Martin, hang our coats in the front closet." She pointed.

Margie beamed as she guided us to the dining room, where plates of food lay on the round table—a great ham peppered over with crumbs, a roast beef, a browned turkey, and even a glass vase with some tall celery stalks. For dessert, there was a dish of custard topped with grated nutmeg and a small bowl of chocolates and sweets wrapped in gold and silver papers. A carafe of hot coffee stood on a counter.

"You've outdone yourself, Margie." My grandmother kissed her cheek. "Thank you for celebrating Laura's return."

"You are so kind," my mother added, and we all took our seats.

Arthur rubbed himself against our legs. He was wearing a paper crown.

Mom picked him up. "King Arthur. How cute!" She fingered one of the gold triangular points and touched the cross on the front. "The power of religion," she mumbled, snuggling Arthur against her cheek.

He squirmed, and my mother put him on the floor.

My grandmother laughed. "Where did you get that thing?"

"A shy little girl was selling them outside of Stop and Shop to raise money for her school."

The doorbell rang.

"I'll get it." Martin ran and returned with Rita and my father, who was pushing his damp hair back. He shivered. "It's getting cold out there." He looked at the table. "Nice spread, Margie."

She blushed. "It's nothin'. Got a caterer from the supermarket."

"Good to see you home, Laura." He hugged her.

"It's great to be out of that place."

We helped ourselves to the buffet, then sat in the living room and talked about the future. My mother told stories about the institution and how she felt bad for many of the patients, especially Nell and the freak accident that ended her life.

"She thought an eagle was chasing me down the hall. Nell grabbed a broom from the cleaning cart and tried to hit it." Her voice shook. "She swung the broom with such force that the wooden pole broke against the wall. A portion of the wood bounced off the wall and impaled her eye." She crossed her arms and held on to her shoulders, continuing in a controlled monotone voice. "The doctors said her brain was damaged." Her gaze was unfocused, as if she was looking into the memory. "The next day she died from a stroke."

"That story gives me the willies." Margie shivered. "Death is horrible. I can't stand the thought of winding up in a coffin for eternity." She grimaced.

"In the olden days, the monks used to sleep in their coffins," Rita said. "Sounds nuts to me."

My grandmother said, "They did it to remind them of their last end." She paused and looked toward the entrance to the kitchen. "Sean?" Her face flushed.

My mother and I followed her gaze. My grandfather wore a white suit and hat, which he tipped at us. He smiled, then vanished.

Rita said, "Why are you calling for Sean?"

My grandmother laughed. "I imagined I saw him watching us."

"This conversation is getting so mortal." Margie spat on her napkin and rubbed a stain off her sweater.

"*Morbid.*" Rita rolled her eyes and winked at me.

"Let's put on some music." Martin jumped up and turned on the radio console. A traditional Irish ballad, "The Lass of Aughrim," played on Margie's favorite station. The rich voice of an Irish tenor sang.

> *Oh the rain falls on my heavy locks*
> *and the dew wets my skin.*
> *My babe lies cold within my arms*
> *but none will let me in.*
> *My babe lies cold within my arms*
> *but none will let me in.*

My grandmother looked preoccupied. We were silent

"Are you OK?" Mom said.

"Your father used to sing that song."

"That's romantic, Ma."

"Yes, it was." She smiled, but her eyes were rheumy.

My skin became icy and numb. Nana would soon be dead. I began to shiver. I saw paramedics taking her body out the front door of her house and down the steps. A white sheet covered her corpse. Martin cried, "I want to see her" and pushed over a chair. My mother held him back.

Goosebumps covered my cold arms.

My mother said, "Are you OK, Aiden?"

Margie said, "Oh my God. He looks sick. I hope he's not allergic to something he nibbled on."

I fell off the chair.

Later, I woke to the touch of Nana's chilled hand on my head. I was lying on Margie's couch in the living room.

"How are you, Aiden?"

"I'm OK." I looked through the doorway. The others were talking softly around the table.

"I think you've had a bit of food poisoning, dear. It can come on suddenly. You look better now." She fluffed the pillows behind my head and examined my arms. "Your skin looks better. The bumps are gone." She put a thermometer in my mouth.

"How is he?" Martin said.

Nana cocked her head to see the mercury. "Ninety-eight-point-two. He'll be fine." She wiped my sweaty hair with a facecloth and whispered, "When you're ready, join us at the table." Her lips turned a purplish blue.

Veins bulged in the skin beneath her temples and cheeks. Her eyes were black sockets. A fly buzzed and stumbled on her right ear. I trembled.

She pulled up the blanket. Through cracked and broken teeth, she said, "Take your time, dear. I'll be just beyond the doorway." She smiled. "Call me if you feel dizzy."

As she walked away, my grandfather followed.

Every few weeks, on a Sunday after church, my father picked Martin and me up for a visit. That day, though, Martin was at swim practice, so I would be with him alone. Any hope of my parents getting back together had diminished a few weeks after Mom's release, when they had seemed so affectionate. He didn't visit like I thought he would. My parents seemed so glad to be with each other at Margie's. I didn't understand.

"Stop hovering," my grandmother said. I was peeking through the sheer curtain of one of the bay windows in the living room.

"He makes me nervous."

"Why would your father make you nervous, Aiden?"

"I never know what to say."

"Sit down on the couch next to me." She wore a hairnet and sipped a mug of coffee. Her face looked drawn. My mother, who was still asleep, had been acting erratic. She was having visions of the ghost man again.

Nana put her warm hands over one of mine. "Tell your father about school, your friends. Ask him about work. He loves to talk about that job." She lit a cigarette and inhaled deeply, then exhaled, blowing smoke rings. "Dry *shite* to me."

"What?" I scratched my cheek.

"*Boring*. I find your father boring." She pushed my hand away from my face. "Stop scratching yourself. It's such a nervous habit."

"You don't like Dad?"

"Of course I like him. He's a good man but a wee dull. Or maybe I'm dull." She laughed. "We have nothing in common is all. He's the total opposite of your grandfather, God rest his soul. He was curious about everything and had the gift of gab. Sometimes I would pretend to fall asleep." She smiled, closed her eyes, and leaned back.

I laughed.

A car honked.

I smoothed my sweatshirt and straightened my jeans.

"Do you think they'll ever get back together?"

She tamped her cigarette, stood, and kissed me on the forehead. "I don't think so, darling. Some things are not meant to be. It's nobody's fault."

He honked again.

"Go on. You look fine. Relax. Discuss the weather. They say we'll have snow today. You're a smart boy. You'll think of something to talk about. Don't forget your coat."

The sky was gray and the air brisk. I was glad my father had the heat on.

"Where's Martin?" he said.

The hot air blasted from the dashboard vent. It felt good.

"He's at swim practice."

"At the YMCA?"

I nodded.

"The miracle of heated pools. It's just you and me, then."

I thought he sounded disappointed. "If you don't want me to come, that's OK."

He put his hand on my head. "Of course I want you to come. We'll have a great time."

"What will we do?"

He checked his mirrors and turned into the street.

"You wanna watch the game?" He rubbed beard stubble and smoothed his dark hair. The skin under his eyes looked bluish.

"What game?"

He laughed. "Football. The Bears and the Packers. We can order pizza."

"Sure." I knew nothing about football and hadn't any interest, but watching TV would suck up time. The games lasted at least three hours. We wouldn't have to say much.

When we passed the roundabout by the police station, he said, "How's school?"

"It's good."

"What's your favorite subject?" He glanced at me, then turned on the wipers. The snow had begun to fall.

"English."

"I was never any good at English. What are you learning?" A red truck whizzed past us. "Did you see that asshole? I almost hit him.

Too many irresponsible drivers. They don't give a shit about other people. Always in a hurry to get places."

"Maybe he's late for work."

He laughed. "On a Sunday? I doubt it . . . Hey, I interrupted you. Tell me about your English class."

"We're reading *Great Expectations* by Charles Dickens."

"He wrote *A Christmas Carol,* right? Never read the book, but I liked the movie. The ghosts of Christmas past, present, and future."

"The ghost of Christmas *yet to come.*"

"Huh?" He wrinkled his nose and rubbed it with the edge of his leather coat sleeve.

"Dickens calls the future ghost 'yet to come.'"

"I get it. What's this book about?"

"A boy named Pip. His parents are dead, and he lives with his bitchy older sister on a marshland in the outskirts of England. His uncle is nice, though."

"That's a weird name for a kid. What happens?"

"I just started it. I'm at the part where Pip meets an escaped convict in the graveyard. This scary man in rags jumps up from behind a tombstone in the marshes and grabs him. The guy orders him to bring food and a file so he can saw the chains off his legs. He threatens Pip if he doesn't follow through."

My father nodded. "I like crime and suspense." He turned the heat down. "You comfortable? I hate the sound of that fan."

We passed the Arnold Arboretum, where Nana took Martin and me. The snow was falling softly on the spruce trees. My father put the wipers on high. I liked the swooshing sound. Snow collected on branches and the grass below.

"How's your mother?"

"She's having visions of that old man again."

He shook his head. "I thought she was getting better." The car slid to the right, and he slowed down. "I know you think she's psychic, but I still find that hard to believe, Aiden." We were on the Jamaicaway, a four-lane parkway, one of the curviest roads in Boston.

"I think she *is* better."

"For Christ's sake, Aiden, your mother thinks she sees ghosts."

"Scrooge sees ghosts."

"That's a made-up story." He turned into the parking lot next to Jamaica Pond. We pulled into a space in front of rippling waves. Snow swirled outside the car.

"Made-up stories can be based on real life."

"There *are* no ghosts, Aiden." He took a cigarette from a pack in his shirt pocket and lit it. "I regret my part in having her released from McCall's. Schizophrenia is a serious mental illness. The nurses and psychiatrists said she wasn't ready. Obviously, they were right." He drummed his fingers on the steering wheel.

"Are you and Mom ever gonna be together again?" I felt my eyes tearing up.

He slid closer on the seat and put his arm over my shoulder. A few ashes dropped on my jeans. I brushed them off. "No, Aiden. Your Mom and me, we have different personalities. We don't mesh."

"Why not?"

He tightened his lips, as if thinking what to say.

"I'm moving to Arizona," he said.

"Why?"

"I met another lady, and there's a good job for me out there."

"What about Martin and me? And Mom?" I pushed his arm from my shoulder. "You're dropping ashes on me."

His jaw slackened. "Sorry, buddy."

"I'm not your buddy."

"Fuck it." He looked in the rearview mirror and put the car in reverse. "Someday you'll understand."

"I understand now."

He laughed. "Aiden, you're a kid. When you get older, you'll realize that what I'm doing is the best thing for all of us." A shiny blue car sped by the exit of the parking lot. "People are crazy. Don't they realize they could lose control in this weather?" My father looked both ways before turning.

"You're going the wrong way."

"No, I'm not. My place is in that direction." He pointed.

"Take me home."

"You don't want to watch the game?"

"I hate football, and I hate you."

"You don't hate me, Aiden. You're angry."

He turned right. We passed the arboretum again. The pine branches drooped with the snow. A father and his son shoveled their walkway.

When we were in front of my grandmother's house, Dad said, "Are you OK?"

I opened the door and stepped onto the curb. "You're irresponsible. You don't give a shit about us, and you want to hurry away."

"You're pissed, Aiden. I still love you. We'll talk about this again when you're not so upset. I planned to tell you and Martin over dinner. I was gonna take you out to a nice restaurant. Sorry it happened like this."

My grandmother and mother were shoveling the front steps. They stopped and looked up.

Mom shouted, "You're home so soon. What happened?"

"Nothing," I said.

My father waved to her, then whispered, "Please don't tell them, Aiden. Your mom's not ready to hear the news."

"Dad, I'm sure she already knows. That's the difference between you and her. You think she's crazy, but she's not. Mom has the ability to see things you can't. You'll never understand. I think you're a sad guy, like that ghost of Christmas past." I kicked some snow. "Maybe I expect too much, or maybe I'll understand someday like you said."

"You won't say anything, right?" He looked like a child and an old man at the same time.

"I won't say anything, Dad." I shut the door and walked toward the steps.

"What the hell happened?" My grandmother wrapped her arm around me. Mom kissed my cheek. I heard my father drive away.

"The streets were getting icy. The snow was falling harder. Dad wanted me home before the roads got bad."

My mother was solemn eyed. "They already are."

Nana said, "My ma used to say, 'Never dread the winter till the snow is on the blanket.' Let's get inside."

We leaned the shovels against the side of the house and walked up the steps. I felt the beating of my heart and the passing of air into my lungs. The smoke of my breath rose and dissolved like eddies in a careless sky.

My father drove onward, streets glistening, snow like piled linen, and Arizona far, far away.

On a Saturday evening a few weeks before Christmas, Martin and I went to a Catholic Memorial dance. The school had dances most every weekend, and Martin and his friends got beer from Blanchard's, a liquor store on Centre Street. We joined his friends Billy, Chuck, and Dan in the parking lot. Finding a buyer for our beer was sometimes a challenge, but most often, a twenty-something guy would take pity on us, remembering his teenage ritual. Paying him an extra five dollars for the favor helped too.

We walked toward the train tracks, Billy sticking his tongue out to catch the falling snowflakes and Chuck breathing heavily from carrying the case of beer.

"You need some help with that?" Martin said.

"Nah. I'm fine."

Chuck stumbled over one of the rails.

"Let me take that," Martin said.

"If you insist." Chuck laughed and wiped his forehead. "I'm sweating like a pig."

Billy said, "You are a pig."

The two punched each other good-naturedly and walked ahead of us, bragging about who would get laid first.

Martin and I lagged behind.

The street alongside the tracks was empty, and our voices resounded in the still air. I felt like we were on a stage set. The lights cast a pink hue on Martin's shiny face. His lips looked purple under a pointy nose. Even his eyes were a different color, a silvery blue, like the foam of a cresting wave.

"I want to tell you something," I said.

"Hey, why are you guys taking so long? We have to get a buzz on," Chuck shouted from ahead. A short distance away, a bonfire illuminated the dark tunnel under a bridge. Kids were gathered around it, though I could not make out who they were. Their shadows danced on the cement walls. They were singing, raising Budweisers, and gulping.

"Keep going. We'll meet you under the bridge," Martin answered.

"Whatever you say," Chuck shouted.

Billy saluted us. "Yes, sir."

A cold wind blew, and Martin zipped the top of his coat.

"Dad's leaving," I said.

"I know."

"He told you?"

"He called the night after you guys went out. He said you were angry."

"Aren't you pissed that he's leaving us?"

"Whatever." He raised his shoulders. "There's nothing we can do about it. It's his decision. His life."

When we reached the fire, the other kids greeted us. Some of them were already drunk. A few were smoking weed in the corner. Martin grabbed a Budweiser for both of us and opened them, then threw the caps into the fire.

"To hot babes," he whispered, raising his bottle.

I laughed.

We clicked our bottles and drank.

The crowd, all guys, sang "We all live in a yellow submarine," becoming louder and more raucous the more they drank. I leaned against the stone wall, feeling apart from the rest of them. I didn't fit in. I knew I would leave West Roxbury someday. I couldn't survive in a community that would never accept me. A tall kid (I think his name was Michael O'Hara) looked at me and whispered something to his buddy, a short guy with a peach-fuzz beard. They laughed.

I felt self-conscious when they stared at me. Standing there, among that crowd of kids, I was a phony. I had to hide my true self. I decided that an inauthentic life wasn't worth living. I would be who I was, no matter what others thought. Leaving this town would give me freedom.

Martin came over and patted me on the back. "Are you having a good time?"

"Yeah. Just thinking."

He laughed. "You think too much. Have some fun."

He pulled me toward the fire. I felt drunk and enjoyed the mindless feeling that overcame me. Faces glowed, seeming overanimated when flame shadows crisscrossed their skin. Eyes teared, as though some of the guys would cry. I attempted to join the conversation but failed. They were talking about people I didn't know. As I grew more inebriated, words became a jumbled mess. The murmur of voices was soft, then loud, rising and falling in the windy night, like breath from a snoring earth.

The page of a discarded newspaper flew into the fire and danced through the air, just missing the face of a quiet boy, eyes half-closed, hands in his pockets. He laughed to himself and whispered, "It's wild. It's wild."

"Whoa!" Martin swiped the paper and stomped on it. The quiet boy didn't notice. The others laughed and pointed at him.

"He's shitfaced," someone yelled.

Billy pulled the collar of his leather jacket against his neck. "It's snowing pretty hard." Outside the tunnel, the snow fell sideways, illuminated by the lampposts. Eddies of flakes rose like mini-tornadoes. I felt sleepy and thought how nice it would be to lie down.

"You OK?" Martin touched my arm.

"A little tired."

"The alcohol. It will wear off." He left me by the wall and moved into the circle.

Someone began chanting, "We hate queers. We hate queers." The other guys laughed and joined in. Martin looked down, shuffling nervously.

"We should head for the dance," he said.

The crowd, an army of leather jackets and scally caps, some with shamrock decals on their brims, walked into the snow beyond the tunnel. Dan and Martin were arguing over which of the Reilly girls was the prettiest. Time moved slower, and the sleepers beneath my feet seemed endless. Chuck and Billy threw stones at a rat darting across the tracks. I watched my feet move forward, listening to the scrunch of snow beneath my shoes. My hands and face were cold, stinging when a swirl of smoky wind blew snow in my eyes.

Someone said, "The bikeys are coming!"

Cops on motorcycles charged toward us. The headlights shone brightly, and the buzz of the motors grew louder.

We ran. I slipped on a rail, and Martin pulled me up. Soon we were at the back of the dance hall. The cops whizzed by. I walked ahead while Martin and his friends laughed about the "close call" and complained about how the cops would probably drink their beer. As I turned the corner, I almost stepped into the back of a long-haired woman in a black coat. Her shoulders were curved forward, and she was laughing.

"So you're going to dance with a girl tonight, Aiden?" Moira said and turned. "I'm impressed."

I felt like I would throw up.

"Don't vomit, lad. That wouldn't be pretty." She cackled and wheezed. A clear fluid dripped from her nostrils.

"Surprised to see me?"

I passed her to join the line by the front door of the auditorium.

"What's the matter? Cat got your tongue?"

I felt a rush of adrenaline. "Fuck yourself, you ugly bitch." I pushed her against the bricks and banged her head against a steel cross that was fastened to the wall. Her body collapsed into a heap of white ashes. A rush of acrid air passed my face, lifting the hat off my head. I slipped on some ice.

Martin rushed over and pulled me up. "You OK?" He touched my forehead. "Looks like you're gonna have a bump. You drunk?"

"No." I looked down. "Do you see these ashes?" I kicked them.

"The snow, you mean?" He stared into my eyes. "You're out of it 'cause you hit your head. And why were you screaming at the wall and smashing into it? Are you upset about something?"

He picked up my hat, dusted off the snow, and placed it on my head. "Let's go inside. It's fuckin' freezing . . .You ready?"

"Yes."

"Those guys can be jerks. What they were saying by the fire. I don't hate anyone."

"I know that, Martin."

"Good." He put his arm over my shoulder.

Chapter Thirteen

When we entered the coatroom, I felt hot. The white light and walls had a sobering effect. The coat check lady scowled and stared into my eyes, which I was certain were bloodshot. I stepped back onto someone's foot.

"Ow! Watch it!"

The girl behind me was red faced, her round cheeks like apples. She wore a pink flouncy blouse with a short skirt. The hemline was bordered with a chain of red circles. She passed me and handed her purple coat to the woman. Her lip curled. "What's the matter with you?" She shoved me.

Martin was waiting for me at the entrance to the gym. Strobe lights flickered on the dancing crowd beyond. Vicki Sue Robinson's "Turn the Beat Around" played.

Billy was dancing with a blonde girl whose hair was cut in the style of Farrah Fawcett. We weaved through the crowd, smelling pot, cologne, and sweat. The DJ alternated between holding his earphones and adjusting the mixer. A string of Christmas lights edged the top of the concrete-block walls. To our right was a table where three girls poured cups of what looked like lemonade for a small line of perspiring kids.

"Will you be OK if I leave you?" Martin shouted.

"Of course."

"Sit over there." He pointed to metal folding chairs along the back wall.

"I'll be fine. Have fun."

After I got a cup of lemonade, I sat down. Two girls a few seats down kept looking at me. The song "Colour My World" played, and the dance floor cleared. Courageous boys walked toward girls who pretended not to notice. After taps on the shoulders and requests to dance, couples formed. Dan and Martin danced with the Walsh twins, two pretty girls who lived up the street from my grandmother's house. I felt proud watching Martin slow dance. He rubbed one of his hands across the back of Kara's dress and winked at me when he caught my eye. I smiled and gave him a thumbs up. Chuck approached two girls who shook their heads politely, but a third accepted. I wanted to dance but felt awkward, knowing I was drunk and reeking of alcohol.

I thought I saw my grandfather standing behind Martin. I stood to look but he vanished. When the slow song ended, "Play That Funky Music" blared. Martin danced faster. I loved his exuberance and smile. Kara giggled as he twirled her around. I laughed—too loudly, I assumed, because the girls who were staring at me earlier looked my way and said something to one another. They moved farther down the line, near a door under a red illuminated exit sign.

I began to zone out as "Stairway to Heaven" played. Are our thoughts misgiven, as Led Zeppelin sang? I considered how mysterious life was, how uncertain we were of its purpose. We all have regrets, secrets, and internal pain—my grandmother's guilt over

Grandpa's death, Rita's self-condemnation for the affair, Margie's insecurity and loneliness, my dad feeling like an incompetent parent, Mom's alienation and torment, my shame about being gay. We are all searching for an elixir to ease our pain, on a quest for the Holy Grail, the chalice that will forgive our perceived sins.

I garnered the courage to ask a girl to slow dance. I hugged her close and thought how odd this ritual was. Intimacy with a stranger. For a few moments, you hold someone tight, feeling their warmth and smelling their skin, and then you part. My dancing was mechanical. I moved my hand in a circular motion down the girl's back because the other guys did. I stepped on her foot once, but she politely ignored my clumsiness. Her hair smelled like peaches. As "Lovin' You" came to an end, I looked at Martin, who was still dancing with Kara. He smiled.

After the dance, the guys we came with dispersed, some with their arms wrapped around girls, others looking defeated, hands in their pockets. They walked across the snow-covered lawn toward the tracks. Dan walked Rose, the other Walsh twin, home, and Martin and I headed up Centre Street toward Christo's Pizza, where we would buy a roast beef sub and split it.

The air was cold, but the snow had stopped falling. A half moon was visible over Saint Theresa's church. The snow crunched under our feet. We walked silently, our breath small clouds in front of us.

A snowplow rumbled and scraped the street. I formed a snowball and threw it at the truck. To my amazement, it hit the windshield. The truck squealed and made a loud swooshing sound as it stopped. A burly man with long hair and a beard got out. He wore no coat, just a sweatshirt, baggy pants, and work boots. He ran toward us.

"He looks pissed. Don't say anything, Aiden."

Then I noticed a chain of metal links in one of his hands.

He grabbed me by the hair. "You think you're hot shit, you little punk!" He pushed my head down and swung the chain before my face. "I'm gonna bash your face in."

Martin grabbed the chain. "Stop! I threw it."

The guy laughed. Ice crystals had formed in his beard. "You did not. I saw this fucker."

"Seriously. It was me."

"OK, then I'll bash *your* face in." He pushed Martin to the ground and twisted his arms behind his back.

"Fuck, that hurts."

"How the fuck do you think smashing the snowplow into a lamppost would feel?"

"Bad," Martin said.

"I didn't hear you." The guy dangled the chain in front of Martin's eyes. "Speak louder."

"I said 'bad'!"

"I didn't hear you." He pinched the back of Martin's neck.

"Ow!"

The man laughed.

"Leave him alone!"

"Admit you threw the snowball!"

"I did."

He spat, let go of Martin, and walked back to his truck. Before he opened his door, he shouted, "Go home. And don't you ever do something that stupid again. Someone could die."

As the truck drove off, Martin wiped the snow from his pants and coat and pushed his wet hair back. He laughed. "That was fun."

"Sorry, Martin."

"The guy was right. He could've swerved off the road."

"Yeah." I looked down.

"Dumb mistakes cause accidents. What if he had died? You would have felt guilty for life."

I felt tears on my face.

"It's OK. Just don't do it again." He hugged me. "It was a good shot, but save it for baseball." He laughed, and I did too.

"Your hair looks funny," I said. "You remind me of Mr. Woodlake."

We were waiting for a traffic light to turn.

"Mr. Woodlake?"

"You know. The hall monitor who always stands in front of my homeroom."

"Aiden, Mr. Woodlake is dead."

"Stop bullshitting me."

"I'm serious. Mr. Woodlake was a swim coach at our school. The only reason I know about him is because my coach idolizes him. He was one of his swimmers."

The light changed, and we crossed.

On the other side, I said, "How did he die?"

"He was eating lunch in the teachers' lounge and had a heart attack."

"Around noon?"

"I guess so. Isn't that when we have lunch? Guess Latin School hasn't changed that much from the fifties."

"He died at twelve-oh-seven," I said.

"If you say so."

We were quiet for the rest of the walk to Christo's. When we were seated in a booth eating our sub, Martin asked, "Did you really see his ghost?"

"Whose ghost?"

"Aiden, you know who I mean."

"Yes."

"This shit weirds me out. But I'm gonna ask you. What did he say to you?"

"He said you're a good swimmer."

Martin laughed. "You're making that up."

"Maybe."

He gave me a questioning look.

"Yeah, I made that up." I didn't want to agitate him. I also remembered how Mr. Woodlake said that Martin needed to slow down when he swam.

"But the part about you seeing his ghost is true?"

I could tell he wanted me to say no. I couldn't lie about that. "Yes. I saw his ghost."

We finished our subs without talking. The mustached old guy behind the counter looked over. "Everything all right?"

"Yeah," I said. "The sub is delicious."

"Good. Good. That's what I like to hear." He glanced at Martin. "You brothers?"

"Yeah."

He smiled. "You remind me of how it was with my brother. We were close." He picked up a tray and moved toward the kitchen in the back.

"Are you still close?" I said.

"Nah," he answered without turning. "That was a long time ago. He died when we were your age. Appreciate what you got." The door swung shut behind him.

Aunt Clara allowed Martin to sleep over. The next day, Nana hollered for us to get up. It was about 10:00 a.m. My mouth was dry, and I could feel my heart beating from a nightmare I couldn't remember. I put on a brown-and-gray bathrobe that had belonged to my grandfather. Martin was sprawled face down, one foot hanging over the left side of his cot. He held a pillow against the back of his head.

"Did you hear her, Martin?"

"Yup," he mumbled.

I smelled fried ham.

"We should go down. She's cooking."

"I'll see you there. I need a minute."

When I entered, my grandmother said, "Where's Martin?"

"He's washing."

She glanced at me. "Looks like you should have done the same. Your hair's a mess." She held a spatula and frying pan in her hand.

"Lift your plate." She placed two eggs on it. "There's nice ham over there." She nodded toward the counter where a heap of meat drained on a plate lined with a paper towel. "And grab the toast. I buttered it already."

As she poured cups of coffee, she said, "You boys need to be responsible."

"What?"

"Don't play dumb." She wiped her hands on her red apron, then prepared a plate for Martin. "Your grandfather's bad habits."

I looked down.

"Wrecked after a night of getting pissed." She looked to the door as Martin entered, adjusting his belt.

"Morning, Nana." He kissed her on the cheek, and her nose crinkled.

"I don't know which smells worse. The Listerine or the beer. Sit down and eat up."

Martin laughed. "Looks delicious. You're such a good cook. Thank you, Nana." He winked at me from across the table.

"Aiden, get Martin and you one of those cups of coffee by the pot. Martin, you grab the cream from the fridge. I'm sitting down. My arse is tired."

She ate nothing as usual, smoking and looking at the clock while we enjoyed our food.

"We have a problem," she said.

Martin put his fork down and wiped egg yolk off his lip and chin. He glanced at me.

"Nana, we had a few beers," he said.

She waved her hand. Her gold bracelet with gemstones for all our births jangled. "I don't care about the alcohol consumption. Be careful is all. I couldn't take it if anything happened to one of you."

The wall phone rang. "*Shite.* That's probably him again."

"Who?" I said.

"Mr. Sloan from the convenience store."

"What's Mr. Sloan want?" Martin squinted and looked at me, as if I might know.

"Shh!" She picked up the receiver. "I understand, Steven. The boys are finishing their breakfast." She motioned for us to clean up. "I'll be there within twenty minutes. How's she doing?"

Martin rinsed our plates and silverware, then placed them in the dishwasher.

"She's very emotional, Steven. Always has been. I think that's why she's so fat. Eats to feed her emotions. I saw a bunch of tubbies on the *Phil Donahue Show* talking about it." She pointed at the used napkins. I threw them in the wastebasket.

"I know her tubbiness is not your problem."

Martin and I laughed. She scowled.

"She's a lonely sort . . . Of course not. I know you're a kind man . . . Thank you. I'll be there shortly."

When she hung up, she said, "Margie's got herself in a pickle. Seems she's been shoplifting from Mr. Sloan for months." She fluffed her hair and threw her apron down the cellar stairs for the washer.

"Aiden, you're coming with me. Put on something decent and wash that face." She took a brush from her pocketbook on the counter. "Take care of that rat's nest." She tsk-tsked. "What a god-awful mess."

"His hair?" Martin asked.

"That too."

"Looks like a bird might fly out," he said.

She tapped our backsides with the brush, then handed it to me. "Get going. And Martin, go right home. Herself will be calling me next. I haven't got time to listen to her malarkey."

As we ascended the stairs, she stared at her face in the mirror, fingering the wrinkles around her eyes and opening and closing her mouth when she applied lipstick. "It's not fun getting old and gray," she mumbled. She powdered her face and snapped her compact shut, noticing me.

"Hurry along, Aiden."

Mr. Sloan was a tall, thin man with a shock of black hair and light blue eyes that radiated intelligence and a no-bullshit attitude. His voice was hoarse and deep. When we entered his store on Centre Street, he was bagging a woman's groceries. She smiled at us and passed by, leaving a trace of lilac perfume.

I always felt claustrophobic in his store. The place was jam-packed—snacks, soft drinks, toiletries, newspapers, magazines, cereals, canned goods, bottled foods like cherry peppers stuffed with prosciutto (Martin's favorite), and an assortment of other exotic foods. The lighting wasn't good, and I frequently bumped into the shelves along the narrow aisles.

"Where is she?" my grandmother said after the lady left.

"In the stockroom." He glanced at the door in the rear. "Before we go in, I want you to know the history." He looked down at me. "Are you sure you want Aiden to hear what I'm about to tell you?"

"Aiden is a wise soul." She smiled. "He can handle whatever you have to say." She rubbed my cheek and folded her arms against her green wool coat.

"I told her I was calling the cops."

"Stephen, why would you scare an old lady?"

His voice rose. "I wanted her to stay until you arrived. She wanted to run away. I thought it best you spoke with her."

My grandmother had a worried expression. Her glassy eyes darted to the door. "She could have a heart attack. All that fat and anxiety is not a good combination."

Mr. Sloan shrugged his shoulders and pushed a hand through his hair. "She's been stealing for months. Chocolate bars, small bags of chips, and Cheez-Its. Pistachios are her favorite."

"She's a sad woman. I'm sure she doesn't mean any harm." Nana put her hand on his forearm.

"Maybe so. But I got a living to make. Look at all this shit." He motioned to the shelves. "Costs money. Not to mention the rent for this place and the upkeep."

I looked at a dead light bulb hanging from a cord and a brown water stain on the ceiling. Nana noticed as well. Mr. Sloan unlocked the door.

"Really, Stephen. Did you have to lock her in? You probably scared the life out of her."

"That wasn't my intention."

The door was stuck. He pushed on it with his shoulder. Something made a loud thump on the other side. A cold wind blew out, and I heard Margie whisper, "Take care of Arthur."

Margie lay on the floor at a right angle from the entrance, her legs splayed and the toppled chair beside her. Her gray-and-white-checkered dress had somehow shimmied up her bulbous white legs. My grandmother screamed.

Mr. Sloan said, "My God!" He knelt down and shook Margie's shoulders. "Wake up! Catherine is here."

Nana pushed him out of the way. He slipped on red pistachio shells and fell into a shelf of mustard. Jars fell. Glass and Gulden's splattered the floor.

My grandmother placed her ear by Margie's mouth, said her name a few times, and checked the pulse in her neck. Then she began CPR.

"Aiden, call nine-one-one."

Mr. Sloan said, "The phone's behind the register." He slipped as he tried to get up. A piece of glass cut his hand, and blood dripped onto the mustard-covered floor.

"Hurry up, boy," he yelled.

After the paramedics arrived and took her body out, Mr. Sloan, my grandmother, and I looked on, speechless. Tears streamed down Nana's cheeks. When the EMTs opened the front door, one of Margie's hands fell from the blanketed stretcher. The fingers were stained red from the pistachios she had been eating while she waited to be freed. What was she thinking in her last moments? Then I remembered her whisper—*Take care of Arthur.* The love of her life, a cat. I felt an overwhelming sadness. My young self had no idea of the heartbreak yet to come.

The coroner ruled that Margie suffered "a sudden cardiac death due to atherosclerotic and hypertensive heart disease." There was a small service at Saint Theresa's church but no wake. Because my grandmother was so shaken up, Aunt Clara arranged a gathering at her home directly following the service. Margie had no remaining family, so some of her neighbors, Rita, my grandmother, mother, father, Mr. Sloan, Martin, Aunt Clara, Uncle Stanley, the children, and I were the attendees. Arthur curled on Margie's blue sweater for the last time in a corner of the dining room. He died a week later. My grandmother said the cause was broken heart syndrome, which I learned was a real medical diagnosis.

There was food and drink, especially pistachios, which Martin insisted be part of the menu. He, as always, tried to comfort everyone by telling stories to make us laugh. We bought a record of the songs from *West Side Story* because Margie had been so proud of her role as Maria in her high school musical. We sat in the living room, silent, as "Somewhere" played on the turntable.

Where was that "place for us" and "time for us," and what was the "way of forgiving"? I've often thought about those words since that mournful day. Can we ever completely forgive ourselves? After the incident, Mr. Sloan seemed to age overnight. People tried to reassure him that it wasn't his fault and that Margie was bound to die prematurely because of her poor health, but words cannot easily soothe a broken spirit. He died a year later after he fell on black ice and cracked his skull.

They say that bad things come in threes. I suppose it's part of the Irish nature, the morbid sensibility of our culture. Three is a number that connotes a beginning, a middle, and an end, but there is no end to catastrophes, tragedies, and problems. They are the substance of life. Life is too accidental for uniformity or balance. Things just occur, and I still wrestle with the idea of why. We've all heard the platitude "It's meant to be." What's meant to be? And who or what determines that?

Shortly after Christmas, which, for obvious reasons, wasn't so joyous—Margie's death, my father's impending move, my mother's fragility—Nana came down with pneumonia. During the week between Christmas and New Year's, she was laid up in bed, hacking, feverish, and weak. But still smoking. Martin often visited, and the both of us took turns bringing the food that my mother prepared. Nana lived on a diet of scrambled eggs, buttered toast, coffee, and whiskey.

One evening when I placed the meal on her lap, she said, "Put more whiskey in the coffee. I have some in the top dresser drawer."

I added liquor, and she picked the cup up with trembling hands. The room smelled of sweat and dusty heat.

"It's hot in here, Nana. You want me to open a window? Should I wake Mom?" I said.

"No. I like the warmth. I want to speak with you about something serious." She inhaled her cigarette. "Are you ready to listen?"

"Yes."

The lamplight reflected in the sheen of sweat on her forehead. She rubbed the back of her neck, then clasped her hands together, so tightly that spots of red appeared on her fingers.

She cleared her throat. "Are you certain?"

"Yes, Nana. What do you want to tell me?" I felt my heart beating.

She looked toward the window as she spoke, purposely avoiding my eyes.

"If anything were to happen to me, you must promise to tell Rita something." She coughed and spit phlegm into a Kleenex, which she placed on the bedside table, alongside several other balls of tissue. Her eyes watered. She exhaled loudly, as if relieving a burden.

"I promise."

"I want you to thank her for talking with me so many times about my ma."

"Why?"

"You don't need to know why, darling." She grabbed both my arms and looked into my eyes. "Aiden, we all make mistakes. Guilt is a terrible thing." She smoothed my hair and gazed at my face. "I want you to realize that whatever choices you make in your life, I love you. OK?" She rubbed my hands. "Remember. You must thank Rita."

"OK, Nana."

She sighed and relaxed into her pillow.

Chapter Fourteen

Aunt Clara allowed Martin to spend the rest of Christmas vacation at Nana's house. One morning, we woke to the sound of voices on the second floor, quickly dressed, and went downstairs. In the hallway outside my grandmother's room, my mother sat on the floor, pale and trembling.

"I heard her scream in pain. When I went to her bed, she was talking to your grandfather. She didn't seem to know that I was in the room. She was delirious from her fever."

Through the doorway, I saw two paramedics lifting my grandmother onto a stretcher. My mother held Martin back. She wrapped her arms over our shoulders and led us down the stairs to the kitchen.

"The paramedics are taking her to the hospital," she said when we were seated at the kitchen table.

"I don't get it," Martin said.

"She's dead, Martin," my mother said. "Your grandmother had no pain."

"Why are they taking her to the hospital if she's not alive?" I said.

"Dr. Rieux needs to pronounce her dead."

"Fuck it. I want to see her." Martin pushed a chair over and rushed toward the doorway.

"Stay here." My mother stood in front of him, arms pressed against the doorframe. Behind her, the paramedics had passed with the stretcher. "Your grandmother would want you to remember her alive."

"But I didn't get to say goodbye." Martin cried, leaning against my mother's chest. Her hands cradled his head.

I felt nothing. In retrospect, I realize I was in shock. I was wooden, frozen, feeling stupor. Over the next year, I would experience the stages of grief—denial, anger, depression, but never acceptance.

Every death clings to us, diminishing bits of our joy, ripping away parts of our history and ourselves. I have never laughed so hard as when I was young, before death became part of my experience.

After the church service, we drove to Saint Joseph's cemetery. I was thankful that the temperature was warm—an unusual 48 degrees for January 2 in Boston. We rode in a limousine provided by the Gormley Funeral Home on Centre Street, a short distance from the church. The silence in the car was uncomfortable. I watched the silver hair on the back of the driver's head; it glistened as occasional streams of sunlight passed through the window. How many times had he participated in this ritual? What conversations had he overheard? What clichés about the dead were exchanged? "She's in a better place." "She was lucky to die at home." "She's in the arms of Jesus now." "God rest her soul."

My mother, father, Aunt Clara, my cousins, Martin, and I looked at one another periodically but said nothing. Cary jumped in his seat at one point and said, "There's my friend Paul" as we passed a doughnut shop. Uncle Stanley, always so silent and aloof, preferred to ride in his own car. We would meet the others at the graveyard.

As we entered the cemetery, Aunt Clara began to sob. My mother wrapped an arm around her and kissed her cheek. Martin patted my knee, as if to say, "It will be all right." Greta stared at her mother, open-mouthed. My father looked through the window at the line of trees—oak, elm, pine, weeping willows. Puddles had formed on the circuitous blacktop road. After a few curves, I saw people exiting cars parked on the edges of the lawn. A steel contraption held Nana's mahogany casket above a hole. The priest, Father Flynn, in a black robe with two gold crosses emblazoned on his chest, stood alongside the casket, which was covered with an assortment of flowers—orange, white, green, and purple. I knew the names of some of them because Rita had taught me—long-stem roses, lilies, mums, bells of Ireland, heather. Father Flynn's assistant, a pimply-faced teenage boy, was arranging papers and a Bible, which he handed to him. People walked slowly across the lawn, trying to avoid muddy patches, their shoes crunching on the remains of dirtied snow.

The driver opened our doors and nodded with solemnity as each of us exited. My father led my mother, followed by the rest of us. Rita, dressed in a long black dress and hat, waved to us from under a large oak tree, its branches creating a shady bower. I pulled my suit jacket close and shivered.

The priest welcomed all of us, spoke of my grandmother's life—her hardships in Ireland, her devotion to family most of all, her work ethic, and her sense of humor. He told a funny story about how she once argued with him about having to say so many "Our Fathers" after a confession. She thought her sins were not so severe. "I'm not arguing, Father Flynn," she said, "I'm simply explaining why I'm right!" People over-laughed, as they do in uncomfortable situations. He ended by saying, "O God, by Whose mercy the faithful departed find rest, send Your holy angel to watch over this grave, through Christ our Lord. Amen." To which the crowd echoed "Amen" and crossed themselves.

"I'd like to read something I wrote for Catherine," Aunt Clara said.

"Come over, dear." Father Flynn guided his assistant out of the way.

She had arranged her hair in a braided French bun. Her lipstick and rouge were too red. The rest of her face was pale. She wore a black dress and held a black purse emblazoned with two interlocking Gs, reminding me of the gold crosses on Father Flynn's robe. She took a paper out of her purse with trembling hands. A breeze blew it onto the ground, and the assistant retrieved it. There were bits of dirt on the side facing us.

She began: "*Bonjour* . . . A life is like a tree. It spreads its roots. From those roots comes a trunk, and from that trunk come branches that reach for the sky, a symbol of the hopefulness of life. Sometimes those branches go left, sometimes those branches go right, sometimes those branches go straight up, sometimes those branches break off, sometimes those branches get hit by lightning, but regardless, the trunk, sturdy and strong, allows all its branches to go in whatever direction they so choose. Catherine, a solid, muscular, thick trunk, wanted only the best for all of us here, the branches of her life—her friends and family. We may not have always gotten along, but I admired her strength, her conviction, her love for family—"

A branch broke and crashed in front of her, tumbling into the hole. People gasped as Aunt Clara fell back into the arms of Father Flynn. Martin tried to suppress his laughter and elbowed me. I laughed.

When Aunt Clara was standing again, Father Flynn said, "That was beautiful, dear. I'm sure Catherine, wherever she is"—he looked up—"appreciated it."

Everyone clapped.

I heard my grandmother say, "*Bonjour*? Muscular? What a bunch of drivel. Herself trying to steal the show. I wish the branch had hit her noggin."

"Where are you?" I said.

The people around eyed me.

Rita put her hand on my shoulder. She whispered, "Who are you talking to, Aiden?"

"Martin," I answered quickly.

"I'm right here, buddy."

We gathered at Rita's house after the funeral. Lots of food and drink. People were talkative, relieved to have the ceremony over with. Martin played some of my grandmother's favorite songs—"Danny

Boy," "Too Ra Loo Ra Loo Ral," and "A Mother's Love is a Blessing."

I managed to speak with Rita alone in the upstairs hallway.

"My grandmother wanted me to tell you something."

"What?" She looked perplexed.

"I don't think now is a good time."

"OK. You'll tell me when you feel comfortable. Let's go back downstairs."

I think she was afraid of what I would say. Whenever I called to arrange a meeting, she had an excuse—lunch with friends, an art class, a meeting of her book club, a lecture. It wasn't until April that I was able to tell her what my grandmother requested.

The rest of winter was gloomy, though my mother seemed a changed person, taking charge of the household, shopping, cooking meals, and spending time with us. I always worried her stable behavior would end. Mom never seemed to fit in. I identified with her, but I had an inner strength, perhaps a bit of my grandmother, that made me less fragile.

At last, Rita and I would meet. On the phone, she suggested we take the subway into the Public Garden in late April when "nature is in its bloom." She said, "Let's sit in the sun and look at the flowers. Won't that be lovely, Aiden?"

I agreed, and before long we were exiting Arlington Street station and entering the park. A patch of tulips—reds, oranges, and yellows—swayed in front of the statue of George Washington. The magnolia and cherry trees were full of blossoms. Daffodils and azaleas were scattered in the muddy grass and along the walkways. Students sprawled out on blankets, mothers with baby carriages passed us, and a few homeless people slept on benches.

"Let's go to the other side of the pond and sit under that gorgeous weeping willow near the patch of flowers." She pointed.

We crossed the suspension bridge and found a space of dry grass. Rita opened her large canvas bag. She spread a purple blanket and placed sandwiches, chips, and bottled water on it.

"These are roast beef with lettuce, mayo, and tomato." She passed one to me. She inhaled and closed her eyes. "Isn't this a perfect day?" She reddened. "Sometimes your grandfather and I came here. We both were fans of Yeats, the Irish poet, especially his poem 'The Wild Swans at Coole.'" She smiled at me. "Would you like me to recite it for you?" She pointed to the swan boats and a pair of live swans. "Seems like the perfect moment."

"Sure."

She began, but I was preoccupied with what I was going to say. I caught the end.

"But now they drift on the still water/Mysterious, beautiful/Among what rushes will they build/By what lake's edge or pool/Delight men's eyes when I awake some day/To find they have flown away?"

"Do swans always fly away?"

"They do. But they often return to their home. Like people."

We sat for a while, enjoying our food and watching people on the grass and in the boats. A family of ducks and the two swans moved in unison across the pond. After a bit, Rita tapped me on the shoulder.

"Tell me, Aiden. What did your grandmother say?" Her face hardened, as if fending off something negative. I realized why it had taken her this long to meet up. She was definitely afraid of what I would tell her.

"She wanted me to thank you."

Rita cried softly. I hugged her.

"Why are you crying?"

"I was so nervous about this meeting. I thought Catherine was still angry with me. My relationship with your grandfather was wrong. I betrayed a friend, and I will live with that for the rest of my life."

"She forgave you, Rita."

"I know she did, but I could never erase her pain." After a bit she said, "What did she want to thank me for?" She pulled tissue from her handbag. "I don't understand."

"She wanted to thank you for listening when she talked about her mother. She appreciated your friendship."

A breeze and the smell of lilies surrounded us. A child pointed at one of the swans and yelled to his mother, "I want to be a white bird."

Rita laughed. "That we could all be white birds able to fly away. Wouldn't that be wonderful?" She crumpled the tissue and put it in her bag.

"Aiden, your grandmother had a secret." A motorcycle zoomed on the street beyond.

"We all have secrets."

"Well said." She smiled.

She looked at the water. "Your grandmother's mother, Sinead was her name. She died tragically. She fell into a well."

I pulled some blades of grass and examined them, debating whether to tell her that my grandfather had already told me the story.

She sighed. "Sinead and your grandmother were out picking berries to make jam. They'd been arguing. Catherine was a young girl, thirteen or so. At that age, mothers and daughters often bicker."

"What were they fighting about?"

"Hold on. I'm getting to the heart of it." She tapped my leg. "Girls can be vain at thirteen, and Catherine told her mother she wouldn't pick berries ever again. Her fingers were stained. Sinead said yes, she would, and it went back and forth like that. They were standing by an old well. As they were arguing, your grandmother dropped the pail. Then a dark horse with golden eyes appeared. Catherine was so astonished that she ran across the field. The horse galloped passed Sinead, knocking her into the wall. The stones crumbled, and she fell to her death."

Rita's version of the story was more detailed than my grandfather's.

"Catherine dropped the rope and called out to her ma. But the well was deep, evening was beginning, and there was no answer from Sinead. She ran back to the village to get help. By the time her father and brothers returned with her, the sun had set. They never found your great-grandmother, and from that day forward, Catherine blamed herself."

"But it wasn't her fault."

"Of course it wasn't. But people aren't rational. We feel guilt for things we have no control over. A restless feeling of guilt was always present with Catherine. She confessed her feelings to me and repented many times. I told her she was absolved. But it was fruitless. She would tell me the story again and again, always seeking absolution and forgiveness. I repeatedly said, 'Catherine, it isn't necessary. You did no wrong.'" She paused. "Aiden, we all carry needless feelings inside, and they can hurt us to the core."

I was quiet, focused on my own shame.

"What's the matter?" Rita touched my hand.

"Just thinking."

"Penny for your thoughts?"

"Thinking how you were a good friend to my grandmother and wondering if I will ever have other friends as good as you or Martin."

"Stay away from the water. It's dirty and cold," a mother scolded her young boy. "You could slip and drown."

"Parents and their children." Rita smiled. "Always the same story. They love, they fight, and they love again." She held my hand. "Forgive others. And don't worry so much, young man."

"Do you think it was a pooka?"

"How do you know about the pooka?"

"Grandpa told me. He said it was an evil spirit that sometimes appears as a horse."

Rita laughed. "And when did your grandfather tell you about the pooka?"

"You know when." I rolled my eyes.

"So he gives you lessons in his nocturnal visits?" She began packing our things. She laughed. "That would be just like Sean. He gabbed about every subject under the sun."

I folded the blanket and handed it to her.

"Aiden, it was simply a horse. A wild horse on its way home. Which is our destination now. Grab my arm."

The sky had clouded, and the air was cooler. Rita moved closer. We passed the yellow tulips under the statue of Washington atop a horse.

Rita pointed at its raised left paw. "I wonder where that pooka's off to?" She looked at my face for a few seconds, mulling something over. "The folk in County Sligo, where your grandmother lived, were convinced the horse was a pooka . . . I don't believe it. And neither should you. It's foolishness and ancient superstition." She wrapped her arm around me. The wind blew tulip petals over the walkway in front of us.

Chapter Fifteen

Martin slept over one night in June. We woke at 1:23 a.m. when a dresser crashed to the floor. He jumped up and turned on the light, which began to flicker. By the dresser, I saw my grandfather, red-faced and agitated. He paced back and forth.

"What's wrong?" I asked my grandfather.

He said nothing and sat on the chair by the telescope, watching us.

Martin answered. "The dresser fell over. Maybe we're having an earthquake." His face was sweating as he placed it upright. One of the drawers had broken. "Fuck!"

I felt a breeze.

Martin said. "It's windy in here. Can you feel it?"

"Lie down," I said. "I must have been sleepwalking and knocked the dresser over," I lied. "This house has drafts."

"You haven't walked in your sleep for years. I thought you outgrew it."

"I guess I didn't."

"Are you OK?" Martin said.

"I'm fine."

Martin looked up. "Why is the light flickering?"

"Old wiring."

"It never did that before."

"There's a first time for everything." I laughed.

"This is freaking me out. How can you be so calm?"

"I like unusual events."

Martin laughed and it seemed to relieve his anxiety.

"Get back in bed." I eyed my grandfather who was looking through the telescope.

Martin turned out the light and returned to his bed, pulling the bedspread up to his chin. The moonlight shone through the window.

"Do you think Dad will ever return?" Martin said after a few moments.

My grandfather walked toward Martin and stood over him.

"Yes."

"What makes you think that?"

"I'm sure Dad misses you."

"He misses you too," Martin said.

"Not like he misses you. Dad doesn't like me."

"Why do you say that?"

"I'm weird."

"You're not weird. Stop thinking that."

"Why do you think he left Mom? She's not exactly normal."

My grandfather gently placed his hand on Martin's heart and whispered a prayer. I tried to make out the words, but he was speaking too softly. I heard the word *home*.

Martin said, "Mom said she's planning to take us to Achill Island to see Grandpa's village."

"When?"

"Within a year. Nana left us a lot of money."

The intensity of my grandfather's stare was disconcerting. His shadowy face shone blue. He kissed Martin's forehead.

Martin rubbed the top of his nose. "Feels weird in here."

I thought of Rita. "There's a rational explanation for everything. Drafty air and an old house with shitty wiring."

Martin laughed. "Do you think Grandpa's watching over us?"

"Always."

"That makes me feel good. Does he still come to you at night?"

I wanted to tell him he was in the room with us now. "Sometimes."

"That's cool," he said.

"Dad is so proud of you. All those trophies from the swim meets."

"Dad's proud of you too. He just doesn't say it. Why do you think he made you that study at the end of our hall? The desk was so big we had to lift it through the window. He knows you like to read."

"I wish they could have gone to therapy and worked it out."

My grandfather had vanished. Why was he so upset?

Martin said, "Mom and Dad are too different. They love each other but are uncompatible."

"I think it's 'incompatible.'"

"OK, Poindexter. Let's get some sleep."

"I love you."

"Love you too."

I dreamed of a choppy ocean, Martin, a seal, and a coming storm. My sleep was restless, as always, and filled with nightmares.

In August, my mother, Martin, and I went to Nantasket Beach in Hull, south of Boston. My mother saved matchbox covers to get discounts on rides at Paragon Amusement Park across from the beach. The day was humid with a slight smell of ozone in the air. A few thunderheads loomed in the distance.

We rode on the white roller coaster, took a train through the dark and "scary" Kooky Kastle, whooshed down the water ride known as Bermuda Triangle, and drove the bumper cars that Martin loved.

Later, we ate hot dogs and cotton candy from stands on the boardwalk. My mother draped her arms over both our shoulders and guided us to a clear spot on the sand. The aroma of baby oil, coconut sunscreen, and salty air surrounded us. The breeze felt good against my skin. Mom let go of Martin to hold her red sun hat and pull up a strap on her white sundress. Martin and I both wore plaid swim trunks, his black and gray, mine green and blue.

"Why do they have to play their music so loud?" My mother pulled a blanket from her cane basket. Elton John and Kiki Dee's song "Don't Go Breaking My Heart" blared. "Martin, help me with this." The two assembled a large blue umbrella and stuck it in the sand.

I smelled popcorn, turned, and saw two kids, brother and sister, throwing pieces at one another. "Stop that!" their mother cried. The young girl giggled and pointed when a seagull swooped down and knocked over their bucket. "Now look what you've done. I'm not buying you brats any more food!" The pot-bellied woman, one hand on her hip, grasped a bottle of Coors Light. The kids laughed and ran toward the ocean, where large waves crested, leaving foam and seaweed in their wake.

"Who's going in first?" my mother said when we were all lying down. "Let me rub sunscreen on you."

After we were completely covered with Bain de Soleil, Martin said, "I'll race you."

I followed him, winding through the crowd, trying not to lose sight of his trunks. Over the ocean, heat lightning flickered on and off like a dying lightbulb.

Martin was at least thirty feet out by the time I reached the waterline. I raised my elbows as I walked toward him. The water was cold. He was swimming farther out. I swam badly, my arms and legs thrashing. An old man looked surprised and jumped out of my way. Ever since I'd seen the movie *Jaws,* I was fearful of the ocean, but seeing Martin wading and hearing him call my name reassured me. He always made me feel safe.

There was a boom of thunder. Martin looked at the sky. He called, "We better head in."

My feet got tangled in something under the water, and I panicked. I felt my legs being dragged by what felt like a horse's mane. "I'm caught in seaweed!" My head dropped beneath the surface of the water. I swallowed and choked. I kept spreading my arms to stay above the water, but the waves had become larger. They crashed in my face. I was moving in a strong current parallel to the shore. My mother screamed to a lifeguard. Martin swam toward me. Thunder rumbled, lightning crackled, and rain pelted my face. I heard children's voices: "Come away, O human child!/To the waters and the wild/With a faery, hand in hand,/For the world's more full of weeping than you can understand."

Martin was about ten feet away, and then he disappeared.

"Away with us he's going," the children said.

I awoke to the voice of a sweaty lifeguard, a boy no more than seventeen: "Aiden, can you hear me?" I brushed away the smelling salts he had placed under my nose.

"Where's Martin?"

My mother was screaming his name by the water's edge. A chain of people had formed from the shore into the water. Police and paramedics pushed the crowd of onlookers back. The woman with the belly consoled my mother. Her children looked tired and frightened.

"Where's my brother?" I said again.

Sweat from the tip of the blond boy's nose dripped onto my cheek. "He's probably farther down the beach. You both got caught in a riptide."

I knew he was lying. Why would the line of people be methodically inspecting the area where we swam?

"The rain stopped," I said.

"Wasn't much. A short downpour while you were out there." He turned and looked at the rescue formation. His eyebrows slanted, and he seemed desperate. The other rescuers too. My mother fell to her knees, put her hands against her face, and sobbed. Her red hat blew down the beach.

Two days later, Martin's body washed up. His wake was held at the Gormley Funeral Home, followed by his funeral at Saint Theresa's Church on Centre Street. We were going through the ritual all over again.

We drove to the funeral home in a limousine. I was in a daze most of the time. My mother seemed catatonic. Aunt Clara, Uncle Stanley, Greta, Cary, and my father (back from Arizona) were silent.

We went inside. The priest led us in prayers. Within an hour, a line had formed in the receiving room. I saw classmates, teachers, members of his swim team, neighbors, and many others I did not know. I hated the smell of all the flowers—funeral sprays and wreaths—red roses, white tulips, pink lilies, yellow gladioli, a variety of carnations, chrysanthemums, and more. Aunt Clara had arranged pictures of Martin on tables throughout the room: Martin as a baby, Martin holding a baseball bat, Martin with three hats on his head (he always loved hats), Martin wearing a black leather jacket with a shamrock pin on its lapel, Martin diving into the pool at a swim meet (at the base of the frame was a plaque that read "Seal," his nickname.)

There were, of course, photos of family gatherings and pictures of him and me alone. In one we stood at the end of the driveway, holding our lunchboxes on the first day of school. We wore cardigan sweaters, his red and mine blue. Under one light, the gold frame of a photo gleamed. On our way to a dance, we stood in front of my grandmother's hutch with her favorite yellow teacups in the background.

People kneeled, said a prayer, and each one offered us condolences, holding our hands, or sharing a memory. One of his teachers told me Martin used to talk of how smart I was, and this brought me to tears. Martin, I always believed, was smarter than me.

I don't think anyone has ever loved me as unconditionally as Martin. He saw goodness in me that I never felt. He gave me confidence when I had none. That somber day, I thought of our nightly conversations, his kindness, his laugh, and his determination to make everyone happy. "Are you having a good time?" he would always ask me.

He was older than I, but I felt as though he were younger. His authenticity and innocence were childlike. Everyone seemed drawn to him. The life of the party, he enchanted people with his stories. I would be in the corner seated quietly on the couch, mesmerized by his magic, the way a serious face would brighten when he spoke to them. He had a gift.

I blamed myself for his death. And then I blamed God for stealing him from us so young. He was just a child. I was angry at everyone and everything. In my twenties, I saw a psychiatrist who gave me antidepressants. Doctor Madden had to switch my drugs because nothing seemed to work. Some of the pills had terrible side effects. I was devastated and acted irrationally, obsessed with death. As a form of catharsis, I began to write. Eventually, I stopped the meds and focused on a strict exercise routine that seemed to make me feel better, though I still have disturbing dreams and experience frequent bouts of insomnia. I tried to ignore my second sight, the flashes of intuition, and telepathy. Knowing glimpses of others' thoughts and seeing parts of their future is too disturbing.

The image of a teacher colleague getting sick, suffering, and dying horrified me. A year later, he was dead. After that, I completely suppressed my visions and intuitions.

Now I avoid people and social situations, spending most of my time alone. I continue to retreat in order to hide from others. I immerse myself in reading and writing, the things I most love. Solitude.

My mother was a different story. She never completely recovered, enduring bouts of depression followed by mania. For years she was in and out of McCall Hospital or various halfway houses. The visions of the old man returned. "He keeps asking to be forgiven," she said. Drawing the ghost was her catharsis. I refused to look at the sketches. The ghost was the focus of all my anger. I blamed him for everything bad that had happened.

Dad collapsed from a heart attack while climbing a mountain in Wyoming. His body was flown back to Arizona, where he lived with his second wife. I didn't attend the services. By that time, we hadn't spoken in years. Rita suffered terribly with brain cancer, a glioblastoma. During the end stages of her disease, I moved in so I could assist her. For a long time, Greta, Cary, and I kept in touch, speaking every few weeks on the phone, but that changed with cell phones. Both of them work in the financial world of Wall Street. I'm sure this disappointed Aunt Clara, who had hoped they would become famous actors, fulfilling a vicarious dream. She and Uncle Stanley still live in the house on LaGrange Street.

Phone calls to loved ones were replaced by texts, and texts were replaced by emojis. How can relationships sustain themselves? We become personas talking to personas, steps removed from our real selves. Do we even know our "real selves"? Scientists tell us we are conscious of only 5 percent of our thinking. What ghosts lurk beneath the surface of human understanding? What secrets lie buried in the human heart? We participate in the illusion of knowing one another.

It has been years since Martin passed. What dreams did he cherish? What secrets pained *his* soul? If honest, I admit I knew him at a surface level, but yet I loved him deeply. Can any one of us wholly know another? We are trapped in the prisms of our consciousness. To others, we are shades—ghosts of Christmas past, Christmas present, and Christmas yet to come.

Like Thoreau, I believe time is merely a stream we swim in. Someday the current of water will slip away, taking us with it, but the sandy bottom, eternity, will remain. We want to remember the past as a separate and golden time. We believe we understood one another then, but I doubt we ever did, and I fear we never will. I am certain, however, of the buoy that saves us—hope. Without hope, we are incapable of promise. And without promise, we are incapable of love.

I work as a high school English teacher, not far from my apartment overlooking Carson Beach in South Boston. Mostly I stay in my classroom and avoid colleagues. I don't want to know their thoughts or see their futures.

Finally, in 2016, I surprised my mother, a sprightly seventy-three-year-old, with her longed-awaited trip to Achill Island. At last we would visit my grandfather's homeland and scatter Martin's ashes in the sea.

She waved to me from the sidewalk in front of a gray three-decker house on L Street, not far from my place. The sun can be intense at 2:00 p.m. on an August afternoon in Boston. Our flight wasn't until 5:50, but my mother was a nervous flyer and liked to get to the airport early so she could have a few "cocktails" to "calm her nerves."

I pulled to the curb. The warm air blew dirt into my eyes when I exited the car. She wore a white sundress with a pattern of green shamrocks.

"It's so good to see you, honey." The brim of her sun hat brushed my eyes when she hugged me. I flinched.

"What's the matter?"

"I like your hat, but I don't think you'll need it much in Ireland. The weather is cool and damp this time of year. Actually, most of the year."

"I know that," she said as I put her two suitcases in the trunk next to my carry-on.

She tried to loosen the wooden knob on the hat's chin strap. "Damn this thing. I can't move it. Or maybe it's the arthritis in my hands."

My mother had always kept in great shape through a life of regular exercise, weight lifting, meditation, and diet, but her hands often ached because of the years she spent drawing.

I loosened her strap. We got in my Subaru and drove away.

"Your car is so clean." She moved a finger over the dashboard and looked at the back seat. She sighed.

"What's wrong?"

"Nothing."

"Say it, Mom."

"I was hoping to see a crumb or some napkins, maybe two Starbucks cups lying on the floor."

I laughed. "Why two Starbucks cups?"

"You need to find a partner. I'm not going to be around forever, and I worry about your being alone."

"You don't have a partner either." The traffic was light. I pushed my visor down to avoid glare. We passed a Stop & Shop, a diner, and a 7-Eleven.

She ignored my comment. "So many people. Look at that old married couple." A gentleman wrapped his arm around his tiny birdlike wife. "I want you to have that," she said.

"The old lady or the old man?"

She laughed. "That's not what I'm saying, and you know it."

"Mom, don't worry about me. I'm fine."

"Everybody needs a companion."

"I like who I am."

She touched my knee. "That's what I want to hear." We stopped at a red light. A mother with two boys crossed in front of us.

"I wish Martin were still alive," she said. "I feel like he was stolen from us. He was just a child."

"I feel the same way."

She turned on the radio. There were reports of a young boy from Kansas who was killed on the world's tallest water slide, an eleven-year-old South Carolina girl dying after contracting a brain-eating amoeba, and Chicago protestors calling for change after a police shooting.

"Why do they have to tell us about all the negative things?" she said.

"Money. Bad news sells."

"What happened to goodness?" she said, half to herself.

"Are you depressed?"

"A bit melancholy. Martin should be with us."

"He is," I said.

"Are you having visions again?"

I laughed. "Not for a long while. You?"

"All the time. They haunt me."

I didn't want to hear about them because she became too agitated when she elaborated.

"He *is* with us, Mom."

"Where?" She looked at the back seat, then put her hand against her chest. "For a moment I thought you saw his ghost in the rearview mirror."

"He's in the trunk."

She laughed. "The urn. How could I forget? Won't it be wonderful to spread his ashes in the sea?" On the radio Sam Smith sang, asking if his loved one could hear his call. His soulful voice told of the hurt he'd been through because he missed them like crazy.

"That's a sign, Aiden." My mother was always looking for signs. "Martin's nearby."

"Always." My eyes teared up.

"Don't be sad, darling. One day you'll see him again."

"But I'll be dead." I laughed.

She took a Kleenex from her purse and handed it to me. We were close to the airport. "We're never dead. Just somewhere else . . . I wish you had a partner to share your life with."

"Here we go again." We pulled into the garage.

She held up her hands. "OK, OK. I'll stop bugging you."

Chapter Sixteen

We entered terminal C for the Aer Lingus flight. As always, the airport was packed. "Follow me closely," I said. "I don't want you to get distracted and lose me."

"Just like your father. Bossy."

Going through security wasn't bad, although it took my mother a few minutes to find her passport. She put her carry-on on the floor and shuffled through her possessions. "I think I placed it under Martin." She handed me the small brass cremation urn, barely over seven inches high and emblazoned with a Celtic knot cross. "Here it is."

People behind us were annoyed. One woman gasped when she saw the urn. "I don't think she should be allowed to take that on, sir. It could be a trick. Some chemicals inside. Maybe a bomb."

"Lady," the handsome TSA worker said to the woman. "Watch what you say. I could have you pulled out of this line."

The woman folded her arms and pressed her lips together.

"It's my son. His ashes. And it's sift proof, according to the airline's rules." My mother handed the passport to the TSA worker. I put Martin's urn in her suitcase and closed it.

It was a large plane—three sets of rows. I was glad our seats were on the side with two seats. Being crammed in the middle section with four seats would be unpleasant, especially since my mother had to frequently use the restroom.

"You can have the window." I placed our luggage in the overhead compartment.

A woman across from us smiled and said, "I hope you don't mind cats. Minnaloushe is my emotional support cat. I'm terrified of flying." She pulled her black sweater over her distended belly, as if to protect her. She looked like a drinker—broken capillaries on her face, seborrhea on her forehead, droopy eyes and skin. Pink bald spots were obvious underneath her unkempt over-processed black hair.

"That's an interesting name. What does it mean?" I said.

"Hell if I know. She was my neighbor Maud's cat. She's gone now."

"Dead?" my mother chimed in, bending over me.

"She passed away last year. I warned her that she was trying to do too much. One of those ultraliberal types. Always had a cause. The one that got her was prison reform. That's where she contracted the TB."

"At least she was trying to help make the world better." I hoped that would end our conversation. She seemed like a talker, and I didn't want to chitchat for over six and a half hours.

My mother returned to looking out the window. I was certain she had made the same assessment. The pilot announced we were number one for takeoff, and the airline attendants explained the safety procedures, demonstrating how to use the seatbelts and oxygen masks and pointing to the emergency exits. A round-faced freckled attendant asked us if we were comfortable assisting in the event of an emergency. We assented.

She continued down the aisle checking the passengers, lifting seatbacks, and telling people to make sure trays were in their upright and locked positions. My mother whispered, "Those uniforms are hideous. Aqua coats with tacky gold buttons? Yuk. And that green scarf looked like it was choking her. Did you notice her blotchy neck? I think she's allergic to the material."

The lady across the aisle, obviously listening to us, said, "I hope you're not allergic to cats."

"We're fine." My mother pulled a sketchbook out of her bag and drew. As always, I never looked—for her privacy and for my ease. She whispered, "I hope she shuts up. Maybe you should order her a drink or two. She'll go to sleep."

Both of us slept a few hours. Then we entertained ourselves. I watched *Manchester by the Sea* with Casey Affleck and *Ouija,* a 60s period piece about a mother and two daughters who unintentionally contact the dead father's spirit while running a séance scam out of their home. My mother sketched and read a novel entitled *All the Light We Cannot See* about World War II.

The food was horrible—a choice of chicken with carrots and peas, stale bread with butter, and a wilted salad or beef with the same sides. Neither one of us finished the meal, choosing instead to drink several glasses of sauvignon blanc.

As the plane started its initial descent and the attendants collected our empty breakfast plates (we ate rubbery egg-filled croissants and drank coffee), clouds emerged and rain pattered the windows. Just as the pilot announced to expect some turbulence, the plane dropped several feet and shook from side to side. The overhead compartments opened up, luggage fell out, and the attendants lost their balance, all the while keeping smiles on their faces. My mother put her hand on her mouth, but that couldn't stop the vomit, which sprayed on the seat in front of her. The alcoholic lady removed Minnaloushe from the crate and pet her while looking at the ceiling. She prayed: "Jesus help us. You are the Alpha and the Omega . . . Holy Moly, what's the rest of the prayer?" she screamed.

My mother wiped the chair in front of her with Kleenex.

"Raindrops keep falling on my head. Ooh aah." The lady said anything to distract herself from her terror. The plane rocked. The pilot was flying higher now, trying to avoid the weather. Eventually, the turbulence was less severe, and the shaking subsided. The attendants walked the aisles, taking barf bags, assuring people (some were crying) that everything was OK now.

My mother sighed. The lady across from us closed her eyes and muttered. The black cat with golden eyes glared at me.

"Martin was looking over you. Did you see him?" my mother whispered.

"Where?" I looked up and down the aisle.

"He's gone now, but he stood there while she was praying," she whispered.

I was still recovering from the thought of us crashing. Hearing that Martin was next to me increased my anxiety.

"That song," I whispered. "Raindrops keep falling on my head. What cat woman was singing."

"What about it?"

"Reminds me of your roommate years ago at McCall's. The one who died so tragically."

Her forehead crinkled and her green eyes moved up and to the right. "Aiden, I never had a roommate."

"You remember . . . Nell."

"Nell was in a room down the hall, near the nurses' station."

The cat hissed. The woman had fallen asleep or she had suffered a heart attack. "Mom, you're forgetting, confused, or something. I'm talking about the day we tried to get you out of that place."

"How could I forget?" She cleaned her face and dress with Dove moisture wipes and applied lipstick. "I was so happy to see you." She snapped the lipstick closed and put it in her bag. "Aiden, you know I have an excellent memory. I am absolutely certain I never had a roommate. I always had private rooms. The only reason I was in that room with the extra bed is because a private room wasn't available. They never stuck me with anyone else."

The cat jumped across the aisle, bit me, and scratched my arms. My mother pressed the call button. The lady across the aisle said, "I'm so sorry." She stood and almost fell on me.

"We're fine," my mother snapped. "Put Minna-whatever-her-name-is in her crate." She passed the writhing cat to the lady.

"Some people are so rude. Never mind them," the lady said to the cat, snuggling it against her cheek. I thought of poor Margie and Arthur. Margie's dead body on the floor of Mr. Sloan's place. I shuddered and felt sad.

By the time we descended, the freckle-faced attendant had wrapped my arms in gauze and given me a coupon for a free drink on my next Aer Lingus flight.

When the attendant was out of earshot, my mother said, "So cheap. They should've given you a free flight."

The plane landed, and people clapped. We were silent. I was uneasy. Why had the cat attacked me? The woman had repeated the same raindrops lyric and "ooh aah" refrain the woman in my mother's room had sung. Was it just a coincidence? What was my mother thinking? She rubbed the tops of her hands when she became nervous. She smiled when she saw me notice. "I can't wait to get off this plane and walk on firm ground."

"I'm not sure we ever walk on firm ground," I said.

At the airport, we rented a compact Ford Focus. Driving on the opposite side of the road would be disconcerting, so a smaller vehicle would be practical in case we took excursions through villages and towns, where the roads were narrow.

The Temple Bar Inn on Fleet Street in Dublin wasn't a good choice. After a few days of street noise and what sounded like bullhorn announcements from a race track or gambling casino, we were glad to drive out of the city. We did enjoy the tourist sites—the castle, the National Art Gallery, the Guinness factory, the shops on Grafton Street, Saint Patrick's Cathedral, the James Joyce House of the Dead across from the River Liffey, and Trinity College, where we saw the Book of Kells. I found the illuminated gospels disappointing. Most of the exhibition consisted of photographs with captions. Only a few pages of the book are shown daily. My mother was fascinated by the medieval artistry—geometric designs, large areas of color, and intricate Celtic patterns.

After four days in the city, we drove routes M4, N4, and N5 to Achill Island on the northeast coast. After four hours, when we had reached a road called Ballinock, my mother said, "It says there's a bridge we cross over." A guidebook lay in her lap. She looked tired and apprehensive—blue circles under her eyes, her wavy auburn hair a mess, and a coffee stain on her jeans. She put on her glasses and bent forward, looking for what we both thought would be a large bridge and river.

"Look." She pointed to the Achill Experience Aquarium and Visitor Center on our left, an aqua building with underwater renderings of sea fauna and flora—vivid blues, pinks, greens, and oranges. "It must have been a small bridge because we missed it."

"I'll go in and ask for directions to the bed and breakfast." I parked.

"Be careful."

I laughed. "Of what?"

"Everything."

We hadn't talked about it, but the events on the plane had spooked both of us. I'm sure she was also feeling a sense of foreboding. The gray, drizzly weather and the cliffs in the distance added to the mood. The thought of finally spreading Martin's ashes in Achill Sound contributed to our pensive states. I tried to convince myself that my fear that we were being haunted by a pooka was ridiculous. Pookas, my grandfather had told me, were shape-shifters.

Was that wild cat an incarnation of the old woman who had menaced me when I was young? And was the pooka behind the curtain that day we tried to help my mother escape? I revisited the memory several times. My mother said she never had a roommate. At the time, I had thought it odd how no one else acknowledged the lady.

I opened the car door. "We head down this road and to the left. They were quite nice. All the Irish seem friendly. I guess that stereotype holds true."

"I wouldn't count on it." She said, "Remember—left, left, left."

She had been reminding me of the correct lane for the entire trip. "I got it, Mom. Have we had an accident?"

"No, but there's still time." She laughed.

We drove up a sloped, gravelly driveway to the inn, a white house overlooking Atlantic Drive with spectacular views of Ashleam Bay. The cottage-style house, with its white plaster exterior and large windows, had been added to over the years, giving the building a cozy zigzag shape. There were cracks in the foundation, and the shale roof lacked a few tiles.

"This is divine." My mother exited the car before me. I was always surprised by her childlike excitement and agility. "Look at those clouds. And the mist . . . And what's that black mountain northward? We must drive there."

"That's Slievemore. At its base is a deserted village." I opened the trunk or, as they call it in Ireland, "the boot."

A small woman with bobbed gray hair, dour faced except for sparkly blue eyes inspecting us, stood in the red frame of the doorway. To the right was a recessed extension of the building. A green sign with the word "Bar" in gold cursive swayed in the wind above a blue door. Along the sides of the inn, large rose of Sharon bushes, leaves moist with rain, moved in the breeze as if waving to us.

"I see you noticed the pub. Jim Kearney is the barman. He'll entertain you with the history of the island, the myths of the wee people and fairies, all the things you tourists like to hear about. The sot's a great source of information. Until about eleven p.m., that is, when he's screwed and bores you to death. Repeating limericks or stories he told you at one p.m. He's mostly full of blarney. Wants a good tip is all."

"One p.m.?" My mother dragged two pink suitcases behind her. They matched the bushes.

"What else is there to do on this godforsaken island but drink? . . . Let me help you with one of those." The woman crept down the stairs, bracing herself on the railing. I didn't think she'd be able to lift the larger suitcase. As she picked it up, I noticed well-developed biceps and prominent blue veins in her white skin, like tiny rivers aching to be free.

As if reading my mind, she said, "Thought I couldn't lift the luggage. I've been dragging people's belongings for forty years. You must be the Glencars." For the first time she smiled.

"Yes. My name is Aiden, and my mother's name is Laura." I extended my hand, but she ignored it and climbed up the steps. "How did you know who we are?"

"You're my only guests."

A spray of rainy wind sprinkled us.

"What an uncommon surname," she said, as if thinking aloud.

"This rain will soak us," my mother said.

"You'll get used to it."

"Will the weather get any better?" she asked.

"Dear, this is lovely weather. The best you're going to get. For those of us who live here, this is a beautiful summer day."

My mother shrugged at me.

Our rooms were small but cute, with old-fashioned wallpaper: in both rooms, uneven patterns of gold geometric shapes over a background of variegated green. I had imagined rooms with walls of severe white plaster like the exterior walls of the establishment and the face of our hostess. She still hadn't introduced herself, and I couldn't remember her name from my internet search for an inn.

My mother crossed her arms and shivered. We entered my room, still talking with the woman.

"I'll turn on the heaters. The dampness is hard to avoid."

"What's your name, by the way?" I smiled at her as I took off my jacket. I motioned for my mother's, but she shook her head.

"O'Malley. Grace. But you can call me Mrs. O'Malley. Everybody does. There must be thousands of Grace O'Malleys in County Mayo. I'm a bloody cliché."

"That's the name of the famous sea captain and pirate. I read about the history of this area while Aiden drove."

"I'm no pirate. I'm not rich. And I'm certainly not a queen. Wouldn't be working my arse off all these years tending to every visitor's whim. I hope you take no offense, but you Americans are the worst. You'll give me no trouble, I presume?"

"Of course not," my mother said.

"And Mr. Glencar." She folded her arms. "Please don't encourage Mr. Kearney. He likes the visitors, especially Americans. He's been saying for years that he's moving to the States. Began talking about it when we were classmates at Dooagh National School. Jim was all palaver then, and he still is. Not a bad man. Actually, quite a good son. Takes care of his paralytic mother. His father was stung by a jellyfish and drowned in Keem Bay when he was just a tot." She plugged in a heater. The shape reminded me of the radiators in my grandmother's house.

"Are there a lot of jellyfish?"

"Yes, dear. Jellyfish, salmon, mackerel, lobster, crab. Even sharks."

"Sharks?" My mother placed Martin's small urn on the dresser. "We won't be swimming in this weather anyway."

"Basking sharks. Harmless to humans . . .You'd be surprised at the number of surfers." She looked through the window toward the bay. "I think they're crazy. All that splashing and being thrown about, but people need to get whatever thrills they can while they're living. All paths lead to the grave."

She noticed the urn and reached to pick it up. "How lovely. Do you keep your jewelry in it?" Her fingers traced the Celtic design.

"Martin."

Mrs. O'Malley's mouth opened. She retracted her hands and wiped them on her gray dress.

"The ashes of my son. He drowned when he was young. We're going to spread them in the ocean. He always dreamed of coming here."

Her eyes glistened. "I'm sorry, Mrs. Glencar. Losing a child is something a mother never gets over."

"Or a brother," I heard myself mutter.

"Yes. Yes . . . I'll let you get settled. You must be knackered. If you're interested, we serve tea at four p.m. on the dot. And breakfast is from seven to nine. No later." She turned to leave but paused and looked at both of us. "You know where I heard your name?"

"No," my mother said.

"A Yeats poem. 'The Lost Child'" She placed a finger on her chin. "Or is it 'The Stolen Child'? . . . We learned it in elementary school. Something about a magical place called Glencar in County Sligo. I can only remember one line and wouldn't you know, we had to recite it every year. Old age is making me dotty: 'For the world's more full of weeping than you can understand' . . . I know there was Glencar somewhere in the verse, but I don't remember how it fits in. I suppose none of us know how it all fits in. Ya know what I mean?"

She shut the door softly behind her.

"So much for Irish hospitality," my mother said. "She's got a nasty disposition."

We sat on the bed and took out brochures I had gathered at the visitor center. She wrote down the places we decided to visit, then said, "Where should we spread his ashes?"

"I read about Keem Bay. Check your guide book."

She flipped through and read, "The most beautiful and least known beach in Ireland." She lay the book in her lap and looked at Martin's urn. "Martin would love that. He was always so adventurous. Remember how he used to quote *Star Trek*?" She laughed.

"Going where no man has gone before," I answered. I got up from the bed and stretched.

"He would love that the beach is not well known."

"Time for bed. You must be tired too."

"More excited than tired," she said.

"I'm gonna crash." I kissed her on the forehead. "See you for breakfast."

Mrs. O'Malley served us a scrumptious meal—eggs, bacon, sausages, mushrooms, potatoes, baked beans, white pudding, and oatmeal. We also ate Irish soda bread and drank good strong coffee. The small table, positioned under an oil painting labeled Ross Castle, County Meath, was covered in a white-and-green-checkered tablecloth. A single yellow rose stood in a thin blue vase. Through the window, you saw a charming stone wall and beyond that, Ashleam Bay. The room smelled like bacon and coffee. In the corner a black woodstove radiated much-needed heat.

"Where are you off to?" Mrs. O'Malley refilled our coffee cups.

She wore a red-and-gold-plaid dress with large white lapels. Her apron was dirty. She was cheerier than the night before.

"We thought we'd rent bicycles and get some exercise. Sitting in a car for long hours causes blood clots." My mother handed me another piece of soda bread.

"Living causes blood clots. You Americans worry too much. You'll want to watch where you ride. The roads are hilly."

"We're headed to Keem Beach." I said.

"I'd advise you not to. The distance is too far. And if you'll pardon me for saying, Mrs. Glencar, you're no spring chicken."

"I take good care of myself. My calves are strong." My mother lifted her leg and pulled her jeans up. "Pure muscle."

"Do as you must. But you might get caught in the rain or blown over by the wind or hit by a car."

"Or pummeled by a meteor," I said.

She frowned. "Can I get you anything else?"

"We're fine." My mother smirked.

"Before you're off today, leave a contact number with the girl at the front desk."

"Our cell phone?" I shifted in my chair, ready to leave.

"Of a loved one I can contact in case you get killed."

"That's a lovely thought for the morning," my mother said.

Mrs. O'Malley, her back to us, paused as she moved to the kitchen. "Dying is part of life. And I want to get paid if anything happens to ya."

She turned. "What are you going to do at Keem Beach? Swim?"

"Enjoy its beauty." My mother wiped her hands with a cloth napkin.

Mrs. O'Malley smiled. "Make sure you dress warm."

"We're driving to the center of town first. Is Sweeney Knitwear any good?"

"If you like overpriced clothing. But you Americans can afford it."

"After we buy clothes, we'll rent bicycles at a place beyond that store," I said.

"McNalley's, you mean?"

"Yes, that's it." My mother rose and wiped her mouth.

"A wheel fell off one of his bikes last year. The tourist, a Brit, ran off the road and hit a sheep."

"How horrible," my mother said.

"Yes. The little lamb was hurt badly. The Brit had to pay Mr. Greaney for the medical bills. She was punctured by the axle."

"Was the Englishman hurt?"

"He broke his ankle. 'Twas a good thing."

My mother's brows lifted. "Why would that be a good thing?"

"For centuries, the Brits have been breaking our backs, our arses, and our necks. But never our spirits . . . One more thing. Watch the animals on the road. I'd hate for another one to be hurt by a careless tourist. Enjoy your day."

During the drive to the town center, my mother said, "She's a bitch. I wonder how she keeps that place open."

"I find her entertaining. Maybe that's part of the charm."

At Sweeney's, my mother bought a brown wool dress from the used clothing section. I purchased black wool pants, a charcoal gray

Irish sweater with a diamond stitch, and a scally cap. The sales girl informed me that the particular stitch represented good luck.

"Diamonds aren't lucky for everyone," my mother said under her breath. She was thinking of my father.

We rented hundred-year-old refurbished bikes at McNalley's— my mother's red with large yellow wheels, mine black, also with yellow wheels. An old-timer from the shop helped me tie them to the roof and, we returned to the inn and changed into our new—or rather, "old"—threads, meeting in the hallway and laughing at our images in the mirror.

"We look like we stepped back in time," my mother said.

Chapter Seventeen

The rain drizzled, but large rays of light broke through the steel-gray cumulus clouds. The air smelled of wet dirt and decay. In one of the windows, Mrs. O'Malley shook her head as we rode our bikes onto Atlantic Drive.

"Am I going too fast?" I called to my mother.

"Don't worry. I can keep up."

Everything I'd read about Achill Island was true. I felt like I was at the edge of the world—the ocean, scattered boulders, rocky cliffs, riotous waves, and a horizon that overpowered. Sheep with spots of paint—green, blue, and red—standing or lying on the knolls to our right, frozen and staring. Fields of bog, streams and pools of water, long grass bending in the wind. Spraying rain, tears on our cheeks. Salty air. Cattle lowing in the fields and the pound of the surf—a heartbeat, eternity. Waves rose and fell. The ocean inhaled, then let go. Seaweed, shells, and rubble pushed onto the shore. The water receded again.

A large goat charged my mother, but she outpaced it. I swerved to avoid it and drove into a ditch.

"My God! Are you OK?" My mother circled back. The goat with black-brown shaggy hair and a white underbelly stood on a ledge of grass above us. The rectangular black pupils of his golden eyes were fixed on us.

"Shoo!" My mother waved at it. "That animal gives me the creeps." The goat was motionless.

"I'm OK. A little dirty, though." Mud caked the knees of my pants and the forearms of my sweater. I got up, feeling pain in my lower back and imagining the bruises that would appear on my shins. I pulled up a trouser leg.

"You're scraped." My mother looked around helplessly.

A lanky boy with a curly black hair underneath a brown-and-white-checkered scally cap sat atop a horse-drawn cart with hay.

"How's it goin' there? You look like you've had a spill."

When he was next to us, he jumped off the cart. His open wool coat revealed brown overalls with short suspenders. The white shirt underneath was buttoned to the top. He had light blue eyes, fair skin, and a thin upper lip. His large ears were red.

My mother pointed. "That goat charged my son."

"Ahh." He looked toward the animal. "We've many feral goats on the island."

"Why is it so still?"

"Frightened is all. Or curious about the Americans before him." He laughed and took off his hat. The wind blew his hair. I couldn't tell if he was sweating or the light drizzle of rain was responsible for the moisture on his neck and the top of his chest area. "What part of the States do you hail from?"

"Boston," my mother said, half looking at him and the goat. "I wish it would run away."

"*Mallach De' ort!*" the boy hollered. The goat leaped and trotted off.

"What did you say?" My mother's face grew pale.

"A bit of blasphemy. I'd rather not say in front of a lady." He brushed hay off his boot. "Did the trick though, didn't it?"

"I don't want to keep you from your work. You must be in a hurry to get someplace," she said.

"No rush." He grinned, exposing a small gap between his teeth. "'God made time, but man made haste.' I have all the time in the world. Especially for strangers in need of help."

My mother reached for his hand. He pulled it away. "It's dirty, ma'am. Been cleaning barns."

"Thank you for stopping. Do you know what time it is?" I could tell her agitation was increasing, but I didn't understand why.

The young man (he wasn't more than seventeen) pulled a chain from beneath his overalls. He lifted the old-fashioned brass pocket watch at the end. It was shiny, with black Roman numerals surrounding the wheel and spring parts in its center.

"You must take good care of that. It looks brand new," I said.

"But it is. A present from my da . . . It's one minute past three, ma'am."

The drizzle turned to rain. My mother looked up. The sky had darkened. A breeze rippled the grass on either side of us.

"We should get going," she said, averting her eyes.

"I won't keep you any longer then. Enjoy your stay. It was my pleasure to meet you." He nodded. Walking away, he muttered, "I feel like I know you well. Good people, you are."

My mother and I hopped on our bikes. He stopped in the center of the road. "One question?"

"Yes?" I turned.

"There are a lot of Irish in Boston, I hear. Is the city as nice as they say?"

"It's beautiful if you can stand the cold." I placed a foot on the pedal.

He laughed. "Weather's not a problem. Look around." He put on his cap and returned to the cart.

I waved as we rode off. My mother was far ahead. Why was she in such a rush? She was always so interested in people. I presumed my accident and the goat had upset her.

We entered the inn and took off our coats. Mrs. O'Malley, wearing a lavender nightgown, was seated in a recliner watching television. She didn't look up.

"Hang your things on the hook by the door. I was wondering where you were."

"We're soaked," my mother said, taking my coat. "And I'm tired."

"I warned you." She took a sip from her glass. "This man is an empty sack." She pointed at the screen. "He's a wanker. All palaver. Mexico will never pay for that wall. She's no better. Much too serious and uppity. Mrs. Pantsuit." She laughed.

We sat on the couch. The air smelled of whiskey. The warmth from the fireplace felt good.

"Grab yourself a drink," she said without taking her eyes off the screen.

"I'm fine," I said.

"Me too." My mother sighed and rested her head on the back of the couch. "It feels so cozy in here."

"Of course it does. You were fools to go out in this weather. Aiden, grab your mother a shot of whiskey. It'll do her good."

"No, no," my mother said. "But thank you."

"You Americans. So worried about what you eat and drink . . . That fat man would do well to worry about what he consumes. And that hair. He should sue his colorist. I think that's what they call them. Isn't it?" She glanced at us for the first time. "You both look like you've seen a ghost. Aiden, take your mum to her room. She needs to rest." She grabbed my mother's hand.

Mrs. O'Malley followed us and opened the door. She lifted her chin. "There's a pot of hot tea on the table. You both could use some. And there's some liquor in the bottom of that cupboard beneath the window. Add just a drop. It'll make you feel better. A wee bit will warm your insides up nicely."

Outside thunder rumbled, and lightning flashed.

She said, "It looks like we'll have a stormy night. Turn up the heater if you like."

"Thank you. You're very kind." My mother poured two cups of tea.

"No problem at all." She smiled and hesitated before leaving. "Did something happen on the road?"

My mother and I exchanged glances.

"Nothing," she said. "You were right. I'm no spring chicken." She feigned a laugh.

I closed the door behind Mrs. O'Malley.

When we were both seated, my mother said, "What do you think happened to Mr. O'Malley?"

I looked at the rain outside and the water forming puddles on the earth. "Maybe there never was a mister. If so, she probably killed him and buried him out there." Thunder rumbled again, followed by more lightning. My mother jumped.

I reached for her hand. "I was joking."

"I know that."

"You seem upset. What's wrong?"

"That young man we met." She looked down.

"What about him?"

"He was your grandfather."

"That doesn't make sense."

She walked toward the heater and held her palms over it.

"Why did you stop believing, Aiden?"

"Believing what?"

"In the other world."

"I haven't ruled out the possibility of ghosts or second sight. But believing those things makes life too complicated. I'm sure the young man was a local. The whole incident distressed you. You're not thinking straight."

"You saw him with your own eyes. You heard him with your ears."

"I don't get what you're saying."

"You've lost faith"

"I believe in God."

Her shoulders sagged. "I'm talking about faith in yourself and in others," she pleaded.

"It's too demanding to accept the paranormal. I feel drained, and life becomes . . . I don't know. Fuzzy."

"Aiden, life *is* fuzzy." She sat on the bed and looked out the window. "I need to tell you some things."

"I'm listening."

She patted the space beside her. "When I was about sixteen, your grandmother told me the story of why she and your grandfather came to America." She hesitated, examining my face.

I sat. "Go on."

"Both came for the same reason. They were poor. Too many siblings. And their futures in Ireland seemed desperate. America was a dream, the cliché land of riches. They didn't know each other in Ireland. Fate brought them together in Boston."

"I know that."

"My mother had a cousin who sponsored her. Her father encouraged her to go. He wanted her to attend college, become rich, and send money home, I suppose." She laughed. "The Irish are dreamers."

"Why did Grandpa come?" I poured more tea, and she came to the table.

She scratched her face. Lightning flashed again. The wind moaned.

"He told my mother that when he was a young man, he met two Americans riding bikes on the road. A mother and a son."

My skin felt clammy. Someone knocked on our door. I rose, hitting the table. My mother wiped up the spilled tea.

Mrs. O'Malley held a basket of scones. "I thought you might like these." Her eyes moved from me to my mother. "You still look a bit racked. Shall I get you some more tea?"

"We're all set," I said.

"I'll leave you alone then." She shivered. "Chilly. You'd be smart to keep the heater on high. I don't want you to have unquiet dreams. Coldness does that to me. Good night." She closed the door.

"She's not so bad." I put the basket on the table.

My mother said, "I'm getting used to her. I wonder how she makes ends meet with so few guests." She bit into a scone. "These are delicious."

"Are you really convinced that guy was Grandpa?"

"Positive."

"How can you be so sure?"

"Your grandmother said one of the Americans had fallen off his bike. The son. Your grandfather was on his way back to the homestead with a cart of hay."

"It could be a coincidence."

"Let me finish." Her face reddened and she pushed hair off her forehead. "The Americans asked him the time. He asked them where they hailed from. They told him Boston. He told my mother he felt he knew them, that they were good people. That's what convinced him to leave for Boston."

"It could still be a coincidence." My jaw felt rigid. I didn't want to believe any of this. I had spent my life trying to avoid the paranormal.

The lights flickered, and the heater buzzed. The air smelled like nutmeg, cinnamon, and musk.

My mother sniffed and looked around. "That's his cologne. My mother kept his Old Spice. She would spray it in her bedroom. She said it made her feel less lonely."

The prickly feeling returned.

My mother placed her palm on the top of my hand. "It worries me that you've lost your faith."

"I told you, I haven't."

"You need to stop avoiding people. You need to reach out."

"Here we go again."

"Please promise me."

"What?"

"That you'll make more friends. That you'll date again. You're not too old."

"I'm fifty-four. Gay men have an expiration date stamped on their heels. Age forty."

She laughed. "That's ridiculous. You've got so much to offer. I can't bear to think of you alone."

"You'll be around a long time. Hell, you can pedal faster than me."

"He lost his pocket watch that day."

"Grandpa?"

"After he helped the Americans."

"What else did Nana tell you?"

"She said your grandfather distinctly remembered it was one past three in the afternoon when he met the pair. He felt it had a significance."

"The time? I don't get it."

"I think I may."

"What significance?"

"I'm tired." She stretched her arms. "We need sleep. Tomorrow is a big day." She was referring to spreading Martin's ashes in Keem Bay.

I hugged her and kissed her forehead. "Sleep well. I don't want you to have 'unquiet dreams.'" I laughed.

Before I closed the door, she said, "That goat was headed toward me. I think it was trying to kill me."

"That's ridiculous."

"It's not. We will leave this island tomorrow and head back to Dublin. We can do more sightseeing in the city."

"But we've paid for two more days."

"Let her keep it. Not that she'd refund the money. And I don't blame her. She's running a business."

"And we haven't seen any other guests." I smiled.

"All the more reason."

"Maybe if she were friendlier, the business would pick up," I said.

"She'll survive. This location is perfect." My mother pulled her bedspread down and fluffed the pillows.

"We all survive."

"Yes, we do . . . Set your alarm for the crack of dawn."

"I'll wake you."

"I'll be up." She removed a nightgown from her suitcase. "I hope the weather clears, and the beach is empty."

"I hope so, too, Mom. Love you."

She blew a kiss, and I shut the door.

When she answered my knock the next morning, my mother beamed. She wore a red silk blouse that matched her lipstick. "The skies have cleared. I know today will be perfect."

"You look like you're going to a party."

"It's a celebration of life." She eyed my sweatshirt. "Why do you always wear dark colors?"

"I don't like to stand out."

She laughed. "A little color would look good on you."

I shrugged. "Let's go," I whispered.

We closed the front door gently and walked to the car, speaking in low voices.

"I hope Mrs. O'Malley didn't hear us." My mother hugged Martin's urn. "I would hate for her to say something negative. She doesn't seem to enjoy life." We glanced at the inn windows and saw no movement.

"Some people like being miserable." I opened the passenger door for her.

I drove onto the road and turned on the wipers. Condensation had formed. Mist rose from grass on either side of us. When we reached a peak on Wild Atlantic Drive, the fog disappeared. Sunlight broke through clouds in front of us and shimmered on the ocean to our left. On our right, the cliff sloped upward, mostly grass in varied hues of green. Jagged rocks and broken stones lay beyond patches of yellow gorse and purple heather. Lowing calves rested on the hillside.

My mother lowered her window. She breathed deeply. "Smell the ocean and grass." The air inside the car was moist. She pointed. "Look at those sheep lying on the edge of the cliff." They stared at us.

We descended to Keem Bay, a valley between the cliffs of Benmore and Croaghaun Mountain. The ocean was calm, dark blue-gray farther out and turquoise near the sandy beach below us. Foam gathered around rocky outcrops in the water.

"It's a magical day to do this," I said.

"Why is that?"

"August eighteenth. Add the digits together. Eight plus one plus eight. You get seventeen. And then you add the one and seven to get eight."

"I don't get it." Her eyes squinted.

"In numerology, eight is the number for infinity. Or paradise regained. The study of magical numbers started in Egypt and Babylon. People have believed in their mystical qualities for centuries."

"I will have to read all about it. You always make me think, Aiden."

Soon we were parked. Hand in hand, we stepped through billowing sea grass, as if weaving an olden dance. She held the urn against her, looking down periodically to avoid stones, twigs, and pools among the rushes. The fading moon seemed to take flight, and a lone star, scarcely visible, grew dim in the lightening sky.

In the breadth of the horseshoe-shaped bay, the air around us grew warmer. Sunrise glossed the sand with light. A flock of brown-gray pelicans flew toward the shore. I hoped a world of troubles would disappear, and our hearts would at last feel peace.

Before we entered the ocean, we took off our sneakers and rolled up our shorts. The breeze blew my mother's hair forward, and I thought of the line from that Irish prayer: "May the wind always be at your back." We were alone on the beach, and that felt good.

When we were waist deep, my mother said, "Say a prayer." Toward the horizon, a school of flying fish sprang from an area of frothy bubbles. A heron landed on the cliff and flapped its wings. I remembered how I'd walk self-consciously in church to receive the sacred wafer. My hands, fingers mingled, pressed against my abdomen.

I began the "Our Father," and she joined me. At the end, I heard myself say, "Martin, please forgive me." I was crying.

"It wasn't your fault, Aiden." My mother handed me the urn and rubbed my back. "Wait for a strong wind, then scatter his ashes." She took the top off and held it tightly against her chest.

The wind came, and I moved the urn from left to right, spreading his ashes on the waves. Martin became part of the ocean.

"Look!" my mother said.

At first, I thought a dog was swimming toward the shore.

My mother said, "It's a seal."

The gray head with its large eyes and snout stuck out of the water. Parallel to us, about fifty feet to our left, the dark body extended five to seven feet under the surface. And then it was no longer a seal. Martin emerged from the sea. He was as we remembered him—jeans, a black leather jacket, and a scally cap.

My mother gasped. "Martin!"

He smiled and waved. My mother and I ran toward him but he vanished.

She trembled. "You saw him, didn't you?"

"Yes." I held her close.

For a while, we stood there. The waves lapped against our, bodies and the wind blew softly on our necks.

"Are we crazy?" I said.

My mother laughed. "If we tell people, they will think we are."

"Maybe we imagined it? The mind plays tricks, especially when you're emotional."

"Aiden, we didn't imagine anything. Martin was letting us know he's happy."

I led her to the shore. A car had pulled up next to ours. A young man wearing a black dry suit removed his kayak from the roof. "Brilliant day for kayak sailing," he said. "Looks like ya found a treasure." He glanced at the urn.

"The real treasure is in my heart," my mother said.

"Amen to that," the man said. He looked toward the bay. "Isn't the ocean stunning? A gift from God." Whitecaps formed on the cresting water, and salt spray moistened our faces.

We chatted some more about the beauty of the cove, then exchanged goodbyes. We got in our car and ascended the hill. I'd like to say the sun burst through the clouds, but it didn't. Rain pounded the roof, the wipers moved back and forth, and the wind howled. I thought of our travels ahead. We would leave Achill Island tomorrow and return to Dublin. And from there, we would begin our journey home.

We managed to avoid Mrs. O'Malley. Both of us were tired, so we agreed to meet up for dinner. I awoke about one p.m. My mother, I assumed, was still asleep. She wasn't in the common area, where Mrs. O'Malley sat watching the television.

"You were up early," she called as I passed by. "Missed a good breakfast."

"We took a ride to the beach to see the sun rise."

I told her we would be checking out tomorrow, and she said that was a shame.

"I won't refund your money, you understand?"

"We know."

"You Americans are so frivolous." She shooed me away. "You're interrupting my shows."

I went to the bar and met Jim Kearney. He was a short man with wiry salt-and-pepper hair. He had dark circles under droopy green eyes. He looked hungover and smelled of alcohol.

"What will ya have?" His breath smelled of cigarettes.

"A beer. I don't suppose you have Budweiser?"

"Nope." He opened a bottle of Guinness and placed it on the bar in front of me.

"Second request for Budweiser today." He leaned back and pulled a cigarette from his shirt pocket. "Ya don't mind, do ya?"

"No."

On the dark wooden shelves behind him were bottles of hard liquor—whiskey, rum, vodka, and gin. A sign above him read, "Good Friends. Good Drinks. Good Times." Through the only window by the end of the bar, the rose of Sharon bush rubbed against the glass. Rain pooled along the mullions. Beyond four tables with chairs, logs in a corner fireplace glowed and crackled, reflecting on the hob. Peat smell filled the air.

"The other person was a young man."

"What other person?"

"The one who asked for a Budweiser. He wanted to thank you." He exhaled smoke.

"How do you know it was me he wanted to thank? You don't know my name."

"It's not too difficult. You and your ma are the only guests. It's Aiden, isn't it?"

"Yes. And you're Jim Kearney."

"Ahh. The bitch has been wagging her tongue again."

I laughed.

"I'm afraid I'll be out of a job soon. Nobody likes her. Always has a puss on her face."

"Tell me about the guy who wanted to thank me."

"A handsome lad about sixteen."

"I should be thanking him. He helped my mother and me when I fell off my bike."

He coughed. "He didn't mention anything about that. He wanted to thank you for keeping your promise."

I laughed. "I didn't promise him anything."

"Were you pissed? Maybe that's why ya fell off the bicycle. Shouldn't drink and drive." He laughed and coughed again. "Ya might have promised him something but don't remember."

"I wasn't drinking."

He reached under the bar. "Said to give you this." He placed the mechanical pocket watch in front of me. It was rusted and dented. "Don't know what you would do with a thing like that. It doesn't work. Stuck on one past three. And it looks like he dug it up. See the bits of dirt under the glass."

A log fell off the grate. Bits of glowing embers dropped onto the stone bottom. Jim put his cigarette in an ashtray. He squatted before the fire and arranged the logs with an iron poker.

"What was his name?" I said.

"Mark. No, not Mark." He paused. "Martin." He stood and wiped his hands on his trousers.

I remembered my promise in the treehouse many years ago. *The two of us. Someday we'll make the trip . . . We'll get to see Achill Island,* Martin had said. Again I felt the warmth of his handshake. "Have a good day," I said. "Charge the Guinness to my room."

"But you've barely drunk it. And we haven't chatted. Stay for a bit. I don't get much company."

"Sorry," I said.

"Don't forget the watch."

I put it in my pocket and left.

Chapter Eighteen

We returned to Dublin. I never told Mom about my conversation with Mr. Kearney or the pocket watch. She had been acting odd, talking about her death wishes and a premonition that she would soon die. I didn't want to add to her unease by relating the mysterious event at the bar.

We stayed in a cute bed and breakfast north of the River Liffey and made daily excursions to tourist sites we missed on our last visit. I tried to cheer her up by bringing her to beautiful city parks—Iveagh Gardens, Saint Stephen's Green, Phoenix Park, and Dubh Linn Gardens behind Dublin Castle. On the plane back to Boston, both of us read voraciously. I immersed myself in the stories of James Joyce and William Trevor. My mother read a novel by Edna O'Brien and another by Maeve Binchy.

When the school year began, I was busy but tried to call her once a week. In one of our conversations, she announced that she and her friend Lucy would be traveling to the Grand Canyon in early November. I told her it was a great idea. Her mood seemed hopeful, and the agitation she experienced after our trip had dissipated.

"You'll be OK, won't you?" she asked at the end of our phone conversation.

"What do you mean?"

"Tell me you'll be OK. I worry about you."

"Mom, I'm fine. You've got to stop worrying so much."

"Do you have someone special yet?"

"You."

"Aiden, don't tease your mother. Are you seeing anyone?"

I misled her. "There's a new hire at our school. He seems like a great guy."

She sighed. "Good. Ask him out . . . He's gay, I assume?"

"Yes. I think so."

"That's wonderful."

I had no interest in Mr. Hanrahan, but I wanted to give my mother hope.

On the third day of her visit to the Grand Canyon, she died. A man lost control of his horse while my mother and Lucy stood at Ooh Aah Point on the South Kaibab Trail. The horse brushed against her, and she fell into the canyon. The pooka again? The lady had sung, "Ooh aah. Ooh aah." *Pookas relay veiled messages about your future,* my grandfather said.

I was devastated. My mother was the last of my immediate family. I felt so alone.

Aunt Clara was a great support. She helped me arrange a small get-together with friends and family to celebrate her life. Clara had collected her drawings and hung them in a room off the hall we rented in West Roxbury. I couldn't look at them. It was too painful.

I took two weeks off from school. When I returned, the staff was gracious and kind. My mother would have loved to know that

Mr. Hanrahan asked me if I would like to go out for a drink sometime. I told him I would think about it.

In December, probably because of my depressed mood and memories of Ireland, or maybe because of my Irish obsession with death, I assigned "The Dead" by James Joyce to my AP literature class. A more appropriate name for the class would have been "Place as many students as possible into a rigorous class because it makes the school look good" literature class. Echoing the story, snow fell outside the classroom window during our discussion. I had a horrible cold. My voice was hoarse, my sinuses were congested, and my temperature was elevated.

"I don't get why Gretel woulda told the guy about her old boyfriend. I think she was trying to make him jealous." Gina, a petite girl with a tiny face and round blue eyes, looked around to see her peers' reactions. Few showed interest in the story. Most hadn't read it. Some stared blankly at me, others looked at their cellphones, and several looked at the snow falling softly outside the windows. I thought I would write an essay about teaching called "The Dead."

"Does anyone have something to say about Gina's comment about *Gretta*?" How many more years would I sit in this chair, gazing at adolescent faces and a bulletin board with posters that read "Grammar matters" and "Read: Knowledge is power" and the faces of Shakespeare, Whitman, and other literary greats?

Robert, whose lanky body was too big for the desk and whose legs I was always stepping over, said, "What's the big deal? I don't care about my girlfriend's old boyfriends. All that guy . . . Hansel?"

"Gabriel," I said.

"Yeah. Him. All he should care about is whether he's still getting it."

Breanna said, "You're a pig." She ran a hand through her red hair and glared at him.

"Just being honest."

"Why do you think Joyce named the character Michael Furey?" I said.

Richard scratched his beard and said, "Because he was furry?"

The other students laughed.

"I thought you said his name was Gabriel, Mr. Glencar," Alex said.

"He's talkin' about the boy singing under the tree." Gina snickered, feeling superior because she, at least, had read the story. "I think he was mad because it was raining."

Patrice shrugged and fingered a braid. "Now I'm really confused. What boy singing under a tree? I missed that part. Who sings under a tree? If I seen a boy singing under a tree, I'd think he was crazy and run like hell."

"I think the snow's turning to ice." Damien lifted his head and looked at the window. "Hear the tapping on the glass?" He smiled and turned his head toward the outside.

For a moment, the students looked through the windows. We all did. We all do, I thought. You spend your life thinking something magnificent will happen. Greatness lies before you. You keep watching and waiting. I thought of their college essays: "I want to be a neurosurgeon and a movie star"; "I'm going to be a professional basketball player"; "I want to become a doctor and open a hospital in

Africa." We believe that our futures are full of possibility, that something wonderful will happen someday. But it rarely does. One day you find yourself, a gray-haired man, teaching in a chilly Boston classroom, with the knowledge that you, too, will pass into Joyce's realm of shades, a distant memory for someone, if you're remembered at all.

"What's wrong, Mr. Glencar?" Angela said. She leaned forward, and her eyebrows drew together. "Don't you want to talk about 'The Dead' anymore?"

"Not anymore, Angela. Not anymore." I closed the book. "The bell's going to ring," I announced. "Everybody can pack up. Push your chairs in."

As the other students left, Angela approached me. "Don't feel bad, Mr. Glencar," she whispered. "It's not your fault. I think you're a good teacher. The story's too full of things that we can't understand."

"Thank you, Angela."

When she was near the doorway, she glanced back at me, checking to see if I was OK.

I smiled.

During the ride home, my car slid a few times on the icy road. My apartment wasn't far, but the afternoon traffic was heavy because the school day was ending. The constant stopping for lights or buses made me sleepy. My cold had worsened. My body ached, and I was sweating from a fever.

Eventually, I pulled into my assigned parking spot. I grabbed my satchel full of essays and walked toward the entryway. I paused to look at the snow falling on the waves of Carson Beach. Another resident hurried past me, mumbling something about the storm. I enjoyed the stillness that snow brought. The cold flakes felt good against my flushed cheeks.

I slid as I stepped onto the curb in front of the building. I hit the cement; my ribs ached. My glasses flew off, and the satchel landed in a puddle.

"I got you," someone behind me said. He put his arms under my chest and lifted me. My head pounded, and I couldn't make out his face until he handed me my glasses. Through the cracked lenses, I saw Martin.

"I told you I would always have your back," he said.

"Martin?"

He was gone. The fever was causing hallucinations, I thought.

I saw my reflection inside the mirrored elevator. A sorry sight. Bent, cracked glasses and a cut on my right cheek. Blood, like a teardrop, slid down my face.

A large box lay in front of my door. I pushed it aside with my foot. My hand shook, so it took me a few seconds to insert the key. I propped the door open with my back and kicked the box over the metal door sill.

The warmth inside the apartment felt good. I hung my coat in the closet and brought the heavy box to the table. I immediately recognized Aunt Clara's handwriting. I used a knife to cut through the tape. Inside was an envelope and a pile of what looked like my mother's drawings.

Aunt Clara's pointy cursive read, "Dear Aiden, I have finished cleaning out your mother's apartment. I was happy to do so. I know your sadness must be overwhelming. At some point soon, you will need to call me so we can decide what to do with all of Laura's things. I have stored them in my basement for now. I thought you might like to have some of her drawings. There are a few from the Ireland trip and some from years ago. I love you."

Tears fell as I placed the pile of her artwork on the table. If only I had shown more interest while she was alive, but I associated her drawings with pain. The rendering of the ghost had caused our family suffering—her stay in the psychiatric facility, my parents' divorce, the separation of Martin and me. I resented all that lay on the table before me, and I had stubbornly refused to look at it while she was alive. She was a good artist, people said, and her work had received awards. I wished I had congratulated her.

My hands shook as I lifted the first sketch, a rendering of the mechanical pocket watch from Ireland. A perfect depiction. Even the time was correct. 3:01. I turned it over. On the back, my mother had printed a verse, "Ecclesiastes 3:1. There is a right time for everything, and a season for every activity under the heavens." The next one showed my mother and me spreading Martin's ashes at Keem Bay. I turned it over. "Romans 8:18: For I consider the sufferings of this present time are not worth comparing with the glory that is to be revealed to us."

In the third sketch, the young Irishman stood in front of his cart of hay. He was reaching for his watch. On the back: "Mark 8:18. Do you have eyes but fail to see, and ears but fail to hear? And don't you remember?" Another: A sketch of Mr. Woodlake and me in the hall at Boston Latin. Again, she had meticulously drawn the timepiece. The hands read 12:07. On the reverse side: "Ecclesiastes 12:7. Then shall the dust return to the earth as it was: and the spirit shall return unto God who gave it."

There were several sketches of flowers, trees, and random people in coffee shops, where my mother liked to spend her time. At the bottom, an older sketch, yellowed and a bit smeared, depicted an old man with glasses. His lenses were cracked and a scar marred his cheek. I looked through my broken glasses at his wounded face. At the bottom, she had written, "Aiden, it's time to forgive yourself." *I am the ghost.*

I slept deeply that night, waking once to see Martin sitting on the edge of my bed. He had placed his palm against my sore chest. He whispered, "Go to sleep, brother. It wasn't your fault. I never left you, and I never will."

When I woke, my fever was gone. My body ached, especially my ribs, but I was happy. Had I dreamed that Martin visited me? Had I hallucinated because I was sick? It didn't matter. I thought of my grandfather's spirit: *The most beautiful experience we can have is the mysterious . . . Whoever does not know it and can no longer wonder, no longer marvel, is as good as dead, and his eyes are dimmed.*

The day was bright and the morning was new.

In every beginning is an ending, and in every ending is a beginning. There is no time between, only eternity. When we pass on, we move into another room. Our departed loved ones are a short distance away—in that room just beyond the doorway. They lean in softly, watching over us, taking turns to check that we are safe, placing unseen palms upon our hearts, whispering loveliness in our ears. They are joyful in our joy. They are sad in our sadness. They laugh as we laugh. And they tell stories. "In the beginning was the Word, and the Word was with God, and the Word was God."

In the other room right now, in this eternal moment, Martin is talking with Grandpa. My father is talking with my mother. And my grandmother is chatting too. Nearby, a line of people stretches backward to the moment of Creation. A symphony of voices, murmurs, and inflections, mingling hands and mingling glances, observing the past, the present, and the future. In this time, at the same time, and for all time.

"The Stolen Child" by William Butler Yeats

Where dips the rocky highland
Of Sleuth Wood in the lake,
There lies a leafy island
Where flapping herons wake
The drowsy water rats;
There we've hid our faery vats,
Full of berrys
And of reddest stolen cherries.
Come away, O human child!

To the waters and the wild

With a faery, hand in hand,

For the world's more full of weeping than you can understand.

Where the wave of moonlight glosses

The dim gray sands with light,

Far off by furthest Rosses

We foot it all the night,

Weaving olden dances

Mingling hands and mingling glances

Till the moon has taken flight;

To and fro we leap

And chase the frothy bubbles,

While the world is full of troubles

And anxious in its sleep.

Come away, O human child!

To the waters and the wild

With a faery, hand in hand,

For the world's more full of weeping than you can understand.

Where the wandering water gushes

From the hills above Glen-Car,

In pools among the rushes

That scarce could bathe a star,

We seek for slumbering trout

And whispering in their ears

Give them unquiet dreams;

Leaning softly out

From ferns that drop their tears

Over the young streams.

Come away, O human child!

To the waters and the wild

With a faery, hand in hand,

For the world's more full of weeping than you can understand.

Away with us he's going,

The solemn-eyed:

He'll hear no more the lowing

Of the calves on the warm hillside

Or the kettle on the hob

Sing peace into his breast,

Or see the brown mice bob

Round and round the oatmeal chest.

For he comes, the human child,

To the waters and the wild

With a faery, hand in hand,

For the world's more full of weeping than he can understand.